Lock Down Publications and Ca$h
Presents

TENDER

Emotions Of A Kold Killa

Written By

Khufu

First Edition 2024

Printed in the United States of America

Lock Down Publications
P.O. Box 944
Stockbridge, GA 30281
www.lockdownpublications.com

Like our page on Facebook: Lock Down Publications
www.facebook.com/lockdownpublications.ldp

Stay Connected with Us!

Text **LOCKDOWN** to 22828 to stay up-to-date with new releases, sneak peaks, contests and more…

Like our page on Facebook:
Lock Down Publications

Join Lock Down Publications/The New Era Reading Group

Visit our website:
www.lockdownpublications.com

Follow us on Instagram:
Lock Down Publications

Email Us: We want to hear from you!

Acknowledgement

We all expressions of The Most High and I would like to take this moment in time to express deep reference of The Most High. Thank you for allowing me to exist! I've escaped death many times over for reasons only known by The Most High and I'm forever grateful. Much love to all my loyal fans and Ca$h for the co-sign. To my fanchinerz homie Truth for keepin' it solid and givin' me different perspectives and my newfound Queen Michelle…I love ya girl! Kream wass poppin' Big Homie? RLM…Militant we stand! 210 Slick wass poppin'? World, Sierra wass poppin'?

Dedication

I dedicate this book to all chapters of love I've experienced and to anybody who ever been diagnosed...Tender!

Rest In Power

Lonetta, Pony Boy, Tela, Tayda, Anita, Man Man

Free Da Real

Jeremy, Quinten Bradley, Jimmy Kewes, C-Rock, Keedy, Trey Plus

"The measure of love is love without measure."

Synopsis

After being betrayed by his first love while in prison, Face grows a callous on his heart and embarks on a slew of meaningless flings. He vows to never give his heart to another until he crosses paths with a feisty beauty who's a little too friendly with the sweetness between her thighs. By the time FACE comes to this realization, he's in too deep.

Face's newfound love is made aware of his tender calculated Kold Killing nature and manipulates it to her advantage. Love and attachment have nothing to do with each other, but to Face their one and the same. Will there be consequences for those that cross that line? Will Face be able to keep his emotions in check? Or will he unleash the fury that's been brewing inside?

The streets are about to found out what's TENDER can quickly turned deadly.

Chapter 1
Remember Me?

"Man…Wassup? You know a nigga gotta get back to the center. Give me a shot of that pussy and quit playin'!" Face exclaimed, slightly agitated.

Face had just done fifteen months in prison for two sale charges and was now serving the remainder of his sentence in a work release center in Fort Pierce, Florida.

"Boy, I can't give you none. My period on, unless you want some bloody pussy," Shay retorted, flashing a devilish grin.

Shay was just an around the way girl who Face used to fuck when there was nothing else going on. Shay was a pretty red bone with dark black, wavy hair, and a nice body. If you didn't know her personally, she'd fool you into thinking that she was wifey material.

"Why the fuck you jumped in my shit if you knew yo' shit was bloody?" Face asked with a screwed face.

"'Cause I wanted to see you!"

"Hoe, you trippin'!"

"Calm down and let me suck yo' dick," Shay pleaded, pulling Face's dick out.

Face obliged and let his seat back while Shay performed. It had been nearly two years since he had any type of intercourse, so Face's dick was extremely sensitive.

"Sssssss…Shit!" Face cried, gripping Shay's hair with his right hand and the seat with his left. His toes curled inside his Jordan Retro's while Shay made love to his dick with her mouth.

"Mmmm...Mmmm...!" Shay moaned while sucking and slurping Face artistically. She was trying to hook Face into cuffing her, even though she knew how vicious he was when it came to women. Shay put Face's entire dick in and out her mouth repeatedly until he came in her mouth powerfully. "Mmmmm...Mmmmm...!" Shay moaned and sucked every drop out of Face until his dick started to tickle.

"Aight! Back up; that's enough," Face declared, prying her mouth away from his dick.

Shay looked at him and licked her lips. "You better not be fuckin' wit deez other bitches!"

"What?" Face replied with an expression of confusion.

"You heard me! This my dick, na," claimed Shay.

"That's how you feel?"

"That's what it is!" retorted Shay; assure of herself.

"Look at what'cha did to my purple jeans. You got saliva all over my shit. Grab my bag outta the trunk for me, please. I gotta change before I get back to the center," Face proclaimed, popping the trunk to his rental.

"I got'cha, daddy," Shay retorted seductively before hopping out to grab Face's bag. "I don't see no bag, daddy!"

Sssscrrrrrr! Face punched the gas and left Shay stranded in a deserted parking lot of a packing house.

***

After leaving Shay, Face had close to thirty minutes to spare, so he decided to stop by an old friend. Face pulled into 27 Circle and headed to the back. When he reached the apartment that he was looking for, his heartrate increased as he parked next to a familiar vehicle. It was the vehicle of his ex, named April. He hadn't seen or heard from her in nearly two years. Face was dangerously in love with April, and everybody knew it. While in prison, word had gotten to Face that April was dating a Mexican, but he refused to believe it. He exited his rental and headed to the middle apartment that belonged to Shonda. Shonda was Face's best friend, Quentin Bradley's sister, and also April's cousin. Shonda always had a crush on Face, but that's as far as that went. Face knocked on the door and placed his hand over the peep hole.

"I'm not opening my door until you move yo' hand!" said the voice on the other side of the door.

Face removed his hand and heard Shonda gasp loudly.

"Oooh, girl, that's Face!" Shonda announced happily.

"Girl, don't open that door," April replied nervously.

Shonda ignored April's wishes and opened the door. "Heyyy, baby!" yelled Shonda who then jumped into Face's arms and wrapped her legs around him.

"Wassup, sis?" implored Face chuckling.

"You look so good," Shonda admitted. Face had a head full of deep waves, a muscular build with tattoos on his baby face. "April in there," said Shonda, pulling Face inside her apartment.

When Face put eyes on April, his heart melted. April was seated on the couch five months pregnant. While in prison, he accepted the fact that April had cheated on him and thought that maybe they could patch things up once he touched down, but after seeing her pregnant, he knew it was over. Face had a seat next to April, who was braiding her cousin Crystal's hair. April trembled with fear, not knowing how Face was taking it.

"Wassup?" Face asked.

"Hey," replied April, afraid to look into his eyes.

Face then inhaled deeply, exhaled and asked the most suckerish shit that any man in his situation could ask. "I'm sayin', like…that was an accident, or you planned that?" Face felt like a sucka the moment the last word rolled off his tongue.

"It was an accident," April quickly replied.

11

This lying ass bitch, Face thought. Right then and there he declared to dog every woman he ran across. He shook his head and stood to his feet. "Where Heman at?" Face asked Shonda.

Heman was Shonda's baby daddy. He and Face used to hustle together before Face went to prison.

"He at work. Why?"

"Let me holla at'chu in the room right quick," exclaimed Face, heading to Shonda's room.

Once in the room, Shonda closed the door. "What'chu want, Face?" She asked with her hands on her hips.

"Aye, Heman still got that pistol I left him?"

"Yeah, why?"

"I need it."

"For what? Didn't you just get out of prison?" Shonda asked concerningly.

"I ain't outta prison yet. I'm at the work release center. I'm not finna do nothin' crazy. Somebody wanna buy the pistol and I need the money," explained Face.

"You better not be lying to me, boy. I know yo' crazy ass," retorted Shonda, grabbing the 9-millimeter from a shoe box and handing it to Face.

"Who April pregnant from?" Face questioned, tucking the pistol in his jeans.

"Jesse," Shonda stated evenly.

"You talkin' 'bout the chico that used to hang around me and Heman?" Face questioned in a tone of feigned surprise.

"Yeah, Heman Mexican friend," Shonda assured.

Face thought about all the times he'd come into Heman's house after hustling and would see Jesse hanging around with April close by.

"What'chu thinkin' 'bout?" questioned Shonda, snapping Face out of deep thought.

"Nothin'. Tell Herman I got thirty days left in work release and I'ma pull up on him when I jump."

"Okay, give me a hug before you go," Shonda stated.

Face hugged Shonda then left the apartment without saying goodbye to April. With fifteen minutes to spare, Face hopped in his rental and headed to Wal-Mart on Okeechobee Road. He parked on the side of Wal-Mart and headed into the flower department. Once inside, Face looked around for a few moments, then approached the cashier.

"Excuse me, sir!" said Face, grabbing the cashier's attention.

"Yes, how may I help you?"

"I'm having a hard time finding the fertilizer," exclaimed Face, scratching his head in confusion.

The cashier came from behind the counter. "Right this way. I don't see how you missed it. It's right back here on this last row."

When the cashier turned around, Face had the 9-millimeter pointed in Jesse's face.

"Holy shit, man," Jesse cried, his voice cracking with his hands raised. "The money in the register, man. Take it," Jesse reason visually shaking.

"You don't remember me?" Face implored, grinding sinisterly.

Jesse didn't recognize Face because he had dreads before he was sent to prison, and Face was now built like a Pitbull. Jesse focused in on Face's face. "Face?"

"Yeah, pussy ass chico!" Face yelled through clenched teeth while smacking Jesse above his right eye, splitting him open with the pistol.

Jesse dropped to the pavement and covered his head.

"Look at me, or you going die a nobody in this bitch next to all this fertilizer and shit! Look!" demanded Face.

Jesse removed his arms from around his head and tried to look at Face through all the blood that saturated his face.

"I ever crossed you?"

Jesse shook his head no.

"Yeah, I know, but'chu snaked me doe? You played up under me, my nigga!"

"It wasn't all me, bro! She came on to me. It takes two, bro," cried Jesse.

Face knew that Jesse was right, but he still wanted to leave something embedded in Jesse's mental catalog. From here on out, whenever the thought of snaking another man crossed his mind, Face wanted Jesse to look in the mirror and think of him. "Yeah, you right!" Face admitted, then proceeded to pistol-whip Jesse into submission. "You mention my name, I'ma kill you before they catch me," warned Face before leaving Jesse semi-conscious.

Face knew that the flower department didn't bear any cameras. He jumped in his rental truck and headed back towards the work release center. Face parked his rental at the parking lot he left Shay in. He grabbed his bike off the back of the truck and rode it to the center.

Chapter 2
Laundry Room

When Face entered the center, he headed to the check-in window to sign in. Ms. Brown, who was a C.O. at the center, sat behind the window bearing an infectious smile.

"Ms. Brown, wassup wit' it?" Face inquired, grabbing the check-in log to sign in.

"Heeyy, King!" Ms. Brown retorted, calling Face by his last name. Ms. Brown was a cute heavy-set woman who was low key crushin' on Face. She always let him pass without searching him.

"I'm tired as hell. I'm finna shower and lay it down," said Face.

"Empty ya' pockets," requested Ms. Brown.

"Yeah, right!" Face chuckled and shook his head. Walking down the hallway, Face patted his pocket and was appalled that he still had the pistol on him. *"I'm trippin',"* he muttered to himself then stopped at the back door to toss the pistol in the dumpster.

There were a few males out playing basketball, but they paid Face no attention. He slipped back inside and took a shower. Thirty minutes later, Face emerged from the shower then entered the room that he shared with two other inmates.

"Young Blood, what it look like?" asked an old head name Big Man.

"You already know. Slow motion, OG. How you?" Face remarked, hanging his wash rag and towel.

"I'm just kickin' back on these slow jamz. Gone get'cha self together. I was just acknowledging you," Big Man exclaimed then put his headphones back on.

Face did his hygiene then laid down in a pensive state. He replayed the events of the day repeatedly until the room door opened with his other roommate walking in, interrupting his thoughts.

"What up, Face?" greeted Long Beach, who was extremely black, standing 6'3".

"Wass poppin'?"

"Let me get a pint of Casamigos, pack of Newport's, and two Al Capone Leafs," ordered Long Beach, pulling out his money.

"Get it out my locker, and put the money in there," retorted Face, then gazed back at the roof in deep thought.

"Damn, lil homie, you good?" Beach asked concerned.

"Yeah, I'm good," Face assured.

"Aight. The money in there. I'ma be out back shootin' ceno."

Beach dapped Face up and left the room. Face's mind flashed pictures of April's stomach, making him sick to his stomach. Face couldn't believe that she betrayed him with a Mexican. He vowed to never love again, if he could help it.

"King! Report to the office, now! I repeat: King, report to the office at this time."

Face drew in a deep breath then exhaled with exasperation. He pulled himself out of bed and made his way to the office. When he made it to the front desk, he leaned in the window and found Ms. Brown grinning with redundancy. "Wassup, Ms. Brown?"

"Boy, calm down. I'on want'chu. Ms. Lundy want'chu in the back. Come in, and gone back there," enunciated Ms. Brown biting on her pen seductively.

"Biting on that pen gettin' me a lil excited," Face pronounced, grabbing his dick as he walked past Ms. Brown.

"We'll see 'bout that later," replied Ms. Brown.

Face entered Lieutenant Lundy's office and closed the door behind him.

"Wassup Lieutenant?" asked Face attempting to take a seat in front of the desk.

"Don't sit in my damn chair! Remain standing!" demanded Ms. Lundy.

Ms. Lundy was a fifty-year-old black woman who had thirty years under her belt. She stood 5'8", long black wavy hair, no stomach, and an extremely fat ass. To be her age, she was incredibly beautiful.

"What the fuck did I tell you? Huh?"

"What'chu talkin bout?" questioned Face.

"I told you be careful how you move. I seen you driving in that rental with no tent. If somebody else would of seen you, you'll be on your way back to prison yesterday," exclaimed Ms. Lundy shaking her head.

When Face first came to the center, he had a meeting with Ms. Lundy, and she peeped his last name looking over his paperwork. She grabbed a scratch piece of paper, wrote on it, then slid it in front of Face. The piece of paper read: *Is Joseph King your people?*"

Face shook his head yes. Ms. Lundy ripped the piece of paper and trashed it. She then told Face that she would look out for him. Joseph King was Face's uncle. He used to be a Correctional Officer and had sexual relations with Ms. Lundy.

"Nobody ain't see me. Relax Lieutenant," retorted Face nonchalantly.

"You too close to home to be playing around," she said standing and making her way around the desk.

"I just had to handle a lil bidness. I'm on chill mode na," assured Face.

Ms. Lundy shook her head in disappointment, loosen her belt, then pulled her pants down.

"Hurry up boy," she pronounced bending over her desk.

Face pulled his semi-hard dick from his gym shorts and primed him up until it was standing tall. Ms. Lundy laid her head to the side on her desk and opened her ass cheeks exposing her meaty pussy from the back. Face spanked her right ass cheek with his dick, rubbed it on her clit, then slid into her warm marinated juices. They both moaned at the same time. Ms. Lundy was twenty-eight years older than Face, but she had some of the best pussy he'd ever had. He pushed deep down in her then held it there for a moment enjoying the feeling of her warm, wet walls around him.

Smack! Face smacked her right cheek.

"Boy sshh!" Lundy warned.

Face pulled out of her until only the head was in, then pushed in her again.

"Mmm…" Lundy moaned.

"Shhit!" cantered Face as he picked up his pace and long stroked her standing on his toes with a dip in his back.

"Ssss…ooow, boy, fffuck!" Lundy cried reaching back in an attempt to keep Face from going so deep in her.

Face slapped her hand away and applied more pressure.

Smack! Smack! Smack! Smack! Smack! Smack!

Ms. Brown could hear the sounds of Ms. Lundy moaning and the sound of her ass clapping against Face's pelvis. She had locked the door, covered the window and started playing in her pussy.

"Ssss…yes. That' it. Beat that pussy. Ssss…Mmmm! I want'chu to beat my pussy the same fuckin way," Ms. Brown moaned through clenched teeth while flicking her clit rapidly.

"Fffuck Lieutenant, this pussy bitin'," cried Face stroking Ms. Lundy aggressively.

She attempted to push Face away again, but he grabbed both of her arms, folded them behind her back and fucked her violently.

"Whoooo, I'm cuming baby…. yes!" cried Ms. Lundy as she creamed all over Face fucking up his Polo boxers.

"Ouuuuw, I'm skeetin' in this good pussy!" Face moaned cuming in Ms. Lundy powerfully.

Ms. Brown had came twice already, wiped herself up and was now back at the front window. Ms. Lundy grabbed some wipes, cleaned herself, then grabbed Face's dick and cleaned him too.

"Why you was so ruff? You got something on yo' mind, baby?" Lundy asked looking in Face's eyes.

"Nah, I'm kool. Pussy was good, that's all," lied Face.

"Umm...huh. You better not tell yo' uncle either."

"I ain't in here for all that," Face pronounced, pulling his shorts back up.

"I didn't mean it like that, King. I'ma leave you my number before you leave. Make sure you keep in contact," stated Lundy straighten up her clothes.

"That's wassup," Face retorted before leaving the office.

When he entered Ms. Brown's workspace, she was smiling knowingly.

"Fuck is you smiling for?" Face questioned.

Ms. Brown used her index finger to motion Face closer. Once he was standing in front of her, she spoke her peace.

"What'chu gone do to keep me quiet?" she implored.

"Tssss..." Face exhaled wiping his right hand down his face.

"Yeah playa, laundry room in thirty minutes," demanded Ms. Brown.

Chapter 3
Alone Time

30 days later…Face left out of the work release center and hopped in a new Nissan Tacoma truck that his sister Sierra had rented and left in front of the center at 6:25 a.m. Face pulled off with Ms. Lundy waving bye in his rearview and all of four thousand he'd made working at the packing house and hustling in the center. He'd just given the Department of Corruption two years of his life for the crack rocks he sold to a CI. Face was given a year for each rock. He was now twenty-two and a free man. When he was around the corner from his mother's house, his iPhone 14 started ringing.

"Wass popping?" answered Face.

"Bra, where you at! Everybody here waiting on you and shit," Sierra informed a little agitated.

"Maaan…sis these folks trippin'!"

"What'chu mean?"

"They screamin' I gotta go to another county. Some shit bout added charges and shit!" lied Face.

"What?" Sierra implored in panic mode.

"It's some detectives in here. They screamin' about some murda charges from back in 2016."

Sierra's mind went back to 2016, and she immediately thought of the rumors that were circulating at the time about her brother's involvement in a few murders.

"Oh, my fuckin' God man!" cried Sierra with her eyes starting to water.

Seconds later, Face was making his way down Ave. S. When he spotted his sister, she had her back to the road standing in the driveway with her hand over her heart. Both sides of the road had parked vehicles scattered about. Face discreetly parked the truck a few houses down and hopped out.

"Don't trip though sis, I'ma beat dem charges," Face assured.

"How the fuck you know that!" Sierra retorted hysterically.

Face walked up with his index finger to his lip letting everybody in front of Sierra know to be quiet.

"Because, I'm motherfuckin' bulletproof nigga!" yelled Face.

Sierra turned around and seen Face standing before her, smiling mischievously.

"Boy!" yelled Sierra popping Face with a combination.

Face blocked every punch she threw.

"Calm down, Layla Ali," clowned Face.

"Nigga! Feel my heart." She grabbed her brother's hand and placed it on her chest.

"Yeah, yo' shit beatin' fast as fuck," Face laughed.

"You had me scared as hell. Come here, boy!" Sierra hugged her brother's neck, and he reciprocated.

All the family and friends clapped and yelled welcome home. Sierra removed a Cuban from her neck and placed it on Face's neck.

"Love you, bra."

"Love you too, lil nigga," he replied smiling.

"Heeeyy, auntie baby!" yelled Face's Auntie Beverly. She hugged Face and kissed him on the cheek.

"Wassup, auntie?"

"You like how I put this together? I got meat on the grill and it's a whole lotta liquor in there. Welcome home, baby."

"Thank you, auntie. You know I love you," Face exclaimed, kissed her on the cheek then pushed off to see who was all at the party.

"Wassup, my dog? What dey do?" Robert greeted dapping Face up.

Robert was a tall light-skinned nigga with dreads. He was a real hustler and could be sneaky at times. Robert was also Face's childhood friend.

"Wass poppin'?" Face implored.

"You already know. I'm getting' this money," Robert retorted going in his pocket to pull out a bank roll.

"I view that," Face said.

Robert peeled off a thousand and handed it to Face.

"Bet that up," pronounced Face.

"Hold up," Robert stated, taking a Cuban bracelet from his wrist and handing it to Face.

"I gotta go, my dog. I supposed to be at Wal-Mart shit. I told dem knuckaz I was goin' shopping," Robert proclaimed pointing to his ankle monitor. "Come fuck with me later, my nigga," Robert said before closing his car door and pulling off.

Face threw his hand up and attempted to walk up the driveway when he heard his name.

"Face, check it out!"

When he turned around, he seen his homie B3 posted in the street with a chick. B3 was from Mississippi, but had moved to Fort Pierce, Florida and caught a dope case. Face and B3 were at the same prison and had become close.

"B3 wassup?" Face greeted dapping B3 up while eyeing the chick who was with him.

"What's happnin' baby boy? You finally out," B3 stated sipping from a Natural Ice can.

"Yeah, yeah!"

"This is Chelle, Chelle this my nigga I was tellin' you about," B3 introduced.

Chelle attempted to do her most seductive model pose, but Face wasn't feeling her.

"Wassup, ma?"

"Heey, nice to meet'chu," said Chelle with a gap-toothed smile.

Under different circumstances, Face would have taken Chelle down, but as he looked around there were too many women at his party to choose from.

"Nice to meet'chu too. Aye B3 I'ma fuck wit'chu later, homie. I ain't even seen my mama yet." Face dapped B3 up and noticed the disappointment in Chelle's face.

"Aight, shid! You know I'm on the third. Make that right on Ave. M. I'm at the first apartment on the right," B3 stated walking off.

"Fasho!" replied Face.

When Face made his way up the driveway, his mother Pandora and little brother named World were waiting on him.

"There go my son!" Pandora sang with her hands on her hips.

"Wassup, Ma?" Face implored hugging his mother's neck. "Where you been at?"

"I was in the kitchen cooking yo' food. Ooow boy you look so handsome," Pandora exclaimed smiling happily.

"Nigga you big as fuck!" World stated, dapping his big brother up.

"Da fuck? Nigga look at'chu!" Face retorted.

Before went to prison, his little brother was a jerking, backpack rapper type. Now, he was tatted up from the face to his toes, had shoulder length dreads and gold teeth, standing six feet.

"Yeah, I'm out'chere! Don't let deez skinny's fool you," World stated gripping a FN that was on his hip.

"I love when you talk dirty to me," Face cantered smiling from ear to ear.

"Boy, go put that mess up! Why you out in the open like that?" Pandora cried.

"Ma. You know yo' son got all kinda smoke out'chere. I gotta make sho his welcome is well protected," World explained dramatically.

"Bye! I'm going back to the house. Love ya son," Pandora said before walking inside.

"We gone talk more about'chu being off the porch later," Face told World.

"Ain't nothing to talk about. I'ma dog!" World stated, showing all thirty-two gold teeth.

Face shook his head up and down then made his way to the top of the driveway where he spotted Terrell. While at work release, Face had ran into Terrell when he was out job hunting. She was working the register at Arby's when he came in and asked for an application along with her phone number. Terrell was a dark, tall beauty with a petite body and snow-white teeth. She had shoulder length hair and a bit of a lazy eye. Terrell had been holding Face down for the last few months of his sentence.

"How you doing, Showtime," Terrell asked with a faint smile.

"Wassup T? How long you been here?" Face questioned grabbing her by the hand and pulling her to her feet.

He hugged her but didn't give her a kiss. Terrell peeped it but didn't make a big deal of it. Face had a way with words and had captured Terrell's heart and mind through the letters he'd written her from the center. So, Terrell was under the impression that they were in a relationship.

"I been here a few hours helping out. I like your mother. Y'all look just alike."

"I appreciate'chu being there for me when I was down," Face expressed. "You a real one, T."

"No problem. You deserve it. So, ahh… Now that you've spoken to all yo' lil fams, do you think that maybe we could get some alone time?" Terrell asked voice soft as falling snow.

Face looked around then back at Terrell.

"Yeah, let's do that," he agreed.

Chapter 4
Conflictual

Face left his rental parked at his mother's and jumped in Terrell's Volvo with her. She drove him through the city to show him that nothing had really changed in the two years that he'd been gone. After enjoying a meal at Hurricanes, Terrell took Face on a walk in the sand at Jetty where she questioned his intentions with her now that he was out. She wanted to know if he was going to stand on everything he had said and written in his letters to her. Face assured her that her heart was in good hands. Several hours later, the sun had disappeared, and Terrell's pussy was wetter than a jellyfish from Face's touch. He had been kissing her while playing with her clit and inserting two fingers in and out of her occasionally, driving her crazy.

"I'm ready to leave, baby," Terrell stated standing while pulling Face's hand.

Face rose from the wooden bench with a visible erection and pre-cum in his briefs.

"Mmmm… all that's for me?" Terrell implored biting her bottom lip while grabbing Face's dick.

"As much as you can handle," he cantered grabbing a handful of Terrell's petite ass as he led her to her car.

"Give me the keys, I'm driving," Face pronounced.

Terrell handed Face the keys then got in the passenger's seat. Face hopped in behind her.

"Where we goin'? I'm so horny," Terrell admitted.

"Just chill, I gotta spot," Face assured starting the car and pulling off.

"What hotel you thinking about?"

"You wit' me ma, relax."

Fifteen minutes later, Face was in Sunland Gardens on Avenue T. He pulled behind some trees on the canal bank and turned the car off.

"Where the fuck you got me at, Face?" questioned Terrell looking around nervously.

"Chill, we good bae," Face assured rubbing between Terrell's thighs to calm her.

"How many of your hoes you dun brought back here?" Terrell inquired with her head tilted to the side.

"Nobody ma," lied Face. "Me and my homie used to fish back here. We good T, just relax," Face advised kissing Terrell passionately.

Terrell reciprocated kissing him back. Face knew that he was out of pocket for bringing Terrell to the canal bank to fuck her. He had five grand in his pocket but refused to spend a cent on any woman. It wasn't nothing personal against Terrell. Face heartlessness was just his new way of life, a defense mechanism to protect his heart. In his mind, all women were the same conniving and sneaky. He felt like it was only a matter of time before Terrell showed her teeth, but he was wrong. Terrell loved him.

After kissing Terrell, Face maneuvered to the back seat and started removing his clothing. Terrell made her way to the back seat and did the same. As soon as she removed her last article of clothing, she leaned over and placed Face's entire dick in her mouth slowly.

"Sssss...damn!" cried Face, grabbing Terrell's ponytail.

"Mmmm...mmmm," moaned Terrell as she worked Face's dick in and out of her mouth at an extremely slow pace. The warmth and wetness of her mouth sent chills throughout his body causing him to lay his head back on the seat with his eyes closed. Moments later, Face pulled Terrell's mouth away from his dick.

"What's wrong, baby?" Terrell questioned already knowing that her head game was enigmatic.

"I ain't ready to nut yet. Lay down for me."

Face assisted, helping Terrell get into missionary position in his back seat. Terrell was 5'11, a little too long to be in the back seat so, she reached an opened the door behind the driver's seat. Her head hung out of the back of the car with her legs open. Face left a trail of kisses up her thighs until he reached a place that made all worries temporarily non-existent. Terrell quivered with anticipation as the heat from Face's mouth stimulated her pulsating clit..

"Hhhh…" she gasped right before Face lips latched on her clit.

He maneuvered like a professional pussy eater, kissing, licking, and sucking Terrell's clit proficiently until she came all over his face.

"Ssssss…. ssshit! Ssss…. Ooooww, what'chu doing to me boy! Daaaamn!" Terrell cried trembling with pleasure.

Before she could recover from her orgasm, Face slid all nine inches in her, prompting her to dig her nails in his back.

"Ummmm…" Face cried feeling the full effect of Terrell's warm, wet and tight canal.

"Oooow, yes," she cried grabbing Face's ass to pull him in deeper.

Face picked up his pace and proceeded to stroke her smacking pussy to a cantankerous rhythm.

"Oh Gawd! Ssss… Ooooooww, yes, daddy!" Terrell cried cuming for the second time.

The wetness and constriction of her pussy walls forced Face to cum simultaneously.

"Ffffuck! Ummm…hhmmm! Damn this pussy wet!" Face admitted stroking Terrell slowly until every drop was extracted from his dick.

Face leaned down and kissed her passionately. When he departed her lips, she stated something that made Face uncomfortable.

"I think I love you, boy."

Face looked Terrell in her eyes and chuckled lightly.

"Lovin' me is conflictual," Face pronounced looking in her eyes.

Chapter 5
Pound Cake

The next morning, Face was up bright and early washing his rental in his mother's driveway with his shirt off when a Charger stopped abruptly at the end of the driveway. First glance, Face thought it to be Task Force until the passenger window rolled down exposing two women.

"Boy! You finer than a muthafucka!" Yelled the passenger.

Face laughed at the woman's bluntness. He dropped the water hose and made his way towards the vehicle. Both women gawked at his physique and the protuberance in his sweatpants.

"Wassup wit'ch y'all?" Face implored looking in the car analyzing which one he was gone take down.

"We just came from Gifford and shit. I had grabbed some weed, so I told my friend to take these back streets, and we ran into yo' fine ass," informed the passenger.

Face viewed the driver who was dark-skinned, thick thighs, a little on the chubby side, and couldn't seem to stop smiling. He then viewed the passenger who looked older, but sexy. She had her hair and nails done to perfection and had a nice figure. Face decided that the passenger was the target.

"Y'all from Gifford?" Face questioned.

"Yeah, but I just moved to Fort Pierce off of Oleander," the passenger replied.

"Oh yeah? What'cho name is?"

"I'm Meka, this is Kiki."

"Wassup Kiki," Face spoke. "I'm Face."

"Heeyy!" Kiki said smiling while gripping the steering wheel.

"How old you is?" Face asked Meka.

"I'm 38," Meka shot back proudly.

"Umm, cougar pussy," Face stated grabbing his semi-hard dick smiling.

"It's good too," Meka assured opening and closing her legs trying to contain the pulse in her pussy.

"Oh yeah? Let me get a slice."

Meka laughed, showing her pretty white teeth.

"You want some of this pound cake, huh?" Meka implored looking down at her fat pussy that sat perfectly in her tight leggings.

Face boldly stuck his hand in the window and grabbed a handful of Meka's fat pussy. He then smelled his hand.

"As many slices as possible," Face pronounced licking his fingers.

"Oooow girl! He just too much," Kiki added.

"I see that," Meka stated wide eyed. "How old you is?"

"Twenty-two," Face exclaimed dropping his phone in her lap. "You doing too much talkin'. Log in, and I'ma hit'chu later," Face demanded arrogantly.

"Twenty-two huh?" Meka implored logging her number in. "I got somethin' for yo' young azz. Call me after eight," Meka asserted handing Face his phone back.

"Aight."

"Bring me a friend," Kiki said sounding desperate.

"I'ma try to look out for you."

"Okay," Kiki retorted, pulling off.

When Face turned around his mother was standing there with her hands on her hip.

"Who was that?"

"Some new booty," Face clowned.

"Boy, I'm serious! Na which one you was talkin' to?"

"The passenger, why?"

"I think I know her. Boy, she is my age," Pandora stated crinkling her forehead.

"Just how I like 'em."

"Just be careful," Pandora warned.

"I'm good, ma. What'chu got goin' on this mornin'?" Face asked walking to cut the water hose off.

"I'm finna go handle a lil bidness, pay a few bills and stuff."

"You need a few dollars," Face asked going in his pockets.

"Boy put yo' money in yo' pocket. You need to buy you a car instead of paying for rentals. You thought about that?" Pandora implored.

"I'ma get one mama. I'm just vibin' right na."

"Well, okay. Guess I'll see you later," said Pandora heading to her car to leave.

"Wassup nigga?" World greeted from the porch with a bottle in his hand.

"What's poppin' nigga?" Face retorted dapping his little brother up.

"Koolin' and shit."

"You drinkin' Remy this early?"

"Take me at another one," said World, taking a shot from the bottle.

"What liquor store open this early?" Face asked.

"You know kuz still be boosting and shit," informed World.

"Who Chere?"

"Yeah. You gone take me?"

"Yeah, tighten up," pronounced Face heading to the truck.

"Hold up. I gotta grab some shit. I'm coming," World retorted heading in the house.

Face hopped in the truck and started the engine. Moments later, his phone rang.

"Yeah?" he answered.

"Hi baby," Terrell greeted.

"Wassup with it?" Face retorted thinking about how good Terrell's pussy was.

"I'm just waking up. I thought about you, so I called."

"I appreciate you calling. How did you sleep?"

"Mmmm! Last night was amazing. I slept so good baby. You think that maybe we can have a repeat, except this time in a bed," Terrell implored laughing.

"When you trying to do that?" Face asked noticing his brother making his way to the truck.

"Anytime today is fine with me," Terrell asserted seductively.

"Aight. I'm with my brother right now, but I'm pull through when I'm done."

World hopped in the passenger's side.

"Okay baby. You need anything?"

"Nah, I'm good ma," Face stated putting the truck in reverse.

"Let me know if you do. I'm finna hop in the shower."

"Aight," Face exclaimed.

"I love you."

Click! Face hung the phone up without telling Terrell he loves her too.

Truth is, he didn't know what love was anymore.

"Lover boy!" World clowned.

"You gotta real nigga fucked up! Love don't live here," Face remarked pulling off. "Chere still stay in the jects?" Face questioned.

"Yeah! Here I got something for you, nigga," World said handing Face a mini-Drako.

"Fuck is this?" Face asked in awe.

"That's a mini-Draco, nigga!"

"Damn! I be hearing niggas rap about deez shits, but this my first time seeing one," Face admitted.

"Welcome back from the Stone Age nigga," World laughed. "You was out here putting niggaz down with .38's and long nose deuce, duece's and shit. We on a new flex na. This how we coming!"

"Nigga them tray eight's deadly up close!" Face defended.

"Maan you point that shit at a nigga, ain't no getting away! Ya azz gunned down!" World explained becoming benevolent.

"We gone see," Face retorted looking over at World and noticing tattoos he didn't catch yesterday.

"Um sayin' wassup wit that Bulls tat on ya neck? All them five point stars and shit?" Face implored.

"9 Trey Gangsta! Kream ain't tell you?"

"N'all, he ain't tell me shit!"

"Yeah, I walk with Kream. He prolly ain't tell you 'cause you was behind that G-wall. Matter fact, he outta town on bidness, and told me to give you his new line when you touch."

Kream was Face's big homie from the Blood set 9 Trey Gangstaz.

"Yeah, he gone have to po' me a drink on that one," Face pronounced pulling into Chere's apartment in the projects.

"Damn, who Porsche truck sitting on Armanis?"

"Nigga, that's Chere shit," World stated hopping out the truck. Face followed suit. "Kuz eatin'," World said opening Chere's front door.

"Who the fuck open my damn door!" yelled Chere coming out of her room.

When she seen Face, her face lit up. Face was Chere's favorite cousin. She knew if she called him to come put a nigga down, he coming no questions asked.

"Wassup, big sexy?" Face greeted smiling.

"Kuz!" Chere yelled making her way over to Face hugging and kissing him on the cheeks.

Chere was a big sexy muthafucka who stayed in the latest designer and kept racks on deck.

"When you get out?"

"Yesterday."

"I missed you! Since you fresh out, I'ma look out for you. Give me two racks and you can have all the designer on my bed. It's all kinda shit in there."

"Hold up! I ain't picked what I wanted out yet, Chere!" A familiar voice yelled from her room.

Moments later, Herman walked out of Chere's room. Herman was Face's hustling partner before prison.

"Face?" Herman implored in shock.

Face swiftly drew the mini-Drake from his sweats.

"Nigga I should lift yo' scalp in this bitch!" Face threatened through clenched teeth.

Out of our instinct, World snatched his FN-57 from his purple jeans and pointed it at Herman's face.

"Wassup bra?" World asked waiting on Face to give the okay.

"Y'all please don't get no blood on my Versace couches and rugs. Kill that nigga outside," Chere pleaded.

"Damn Face, wassup?" Herman asked confused with his hands in the air.

Face walked up on Herman until he could feel him breathing on his face.

"Nigga! If you was in prison, you think I'll let one of my niggas fuck on Shonda?"

"Bra, what'chu expected me to do? Be on pussy and dick patrol?"

Face placed the Drako under Herman's chin. "Pussy nigga! She got pregnant under yo' roof! You was supposed to remain loyal to yo' nigga!"

"Kuz!" Chere yelled.

Face looked at Chere then back at Herman.

"Not over no pussy, kuz," Chere stated.

"If it wasn't for Shonda and Quinten, nigga I'll wipe yo' ass down in this bitch. Get the fuck out, nigga!" Face demanded.

Herman pulled away slowly with his hands still in the air and made his way to the door. When he turned to leave, World shot him in his ass.

"Ahhh.. shit!" cried Herman as he ran outside in his Regal.

"Y'all gone bring them Krakaz to my shit! I got too much shit in here kuz!"

"Relax fam, the nigga gone," Face exclaimed tucking his weapon.

World did the same.

"Na, show me this designer shit you was holling about," Face asserted calmly as if nothing had happened.

Chere just shook her head, "Welcome home kuz."

Chapter 6
You Crazy

Kiki opened the door to let Face into the apartment.

"Heeyy Face," Kiki greeted cheerfully, happy to see him.

"Wassup Kiki," he retorted entering the apartment to a detectable stench.

Kiki looked at Face then glanced outside before closing the door.

"I thought you was going bring me a friend, friend," cried Kiki.

"I tried Keash, but all them niggas tied up," Kiki smiled at the nickname he'd given her, and the way he'd said it.

The tone of his voice made her pussy throb.

"Well, I appreciate the effort, friend," Kiki asserted having a seat on Meka's red leather and suede sectional couch.

She grabbed a blunt from the cup holder and put flame to it.

"Don't trip though, I got'chu," Face assured winking his eye at Kiki.

"Fasho friend."

"Where's Meka at?" Face questioned.

"I'm in here, sexy!" Meka answered from the kitchen.

When Face made his way to the kitchen, Meka was standing over the stove cooking in an all-white belly shirt and some white biker tights. When she turned around, her pussy print was so fat and poise that the hair on Face's arms rose.

"You gone speak or just look at my pussy all night?" Meka implored grinning.

"Damn," Face stated above a whisper. "How you doin', Ms. Lady?"

"I'm good. Have a seat. You hungry?"

"What'chu whippin' up?" Face asked looking at all the grocery Meka had all over the kitchen.

It was enough to feed the village.

"Dirty rice, brown stewed chicken, and mac-n-cheese," Meka informed, her ass jiggling elegantly as she stirred the pot.

"Yeah, let me see what'chu taste like," Face remarked as his phone rang.

"Me or my food?"

"Both!"

"Mmmm! I got'chu, lil daddy."

"Hello?" Face answered.

"Hey baby!" Terrell exclaimed excitedly.

"Wassup with it?"

"I thought you was coming to see me today. Where you at? I miss you," cried Terrell.

"I was with my brother, shopping and shit. We finna go to the club."

Terrell exhaled disappointingly.

"Well, okay. Just be careful please! You know how these niggas get round here," Terrell stressed.

"I'm good. Trust me."

"In the morning, come by. I'm cooking you an exclusive breakfast," announced Terrell.

"Okay, I'll be there," Face assured.

"See you then. Love you."

"Aight, ma. Love you too," Face retorted as if he was talking to his mother. *Click!*

Kiki walked in the kitchen and offered the blunt to Face. He took it, hit it twice, and gave it back.

"You good," Kiki asked.

"Yeah. I just got out. I can't smoke too much of that shit right na."

"Aight," replied Kiki heading back to the living room.

"You goin to the club tonight," Meka asked standing pigeon toed as her pussy robbed Face's attention.

"N'all."

"So, I take it that wasn't yo' mother you was talking to."

"N'all that was a lil friend," Face replied gawking at Meka's appearance.

"Why you looking at me like that?" Meka implored with her hands on her soft curvy hips.

"You look like Regina King," Face admitted.

"Is that a good or bad thing?" Meka retorted sitting in Face's lap.

"I love Regina King."

Meka blushed.

"You wanna eat now or later?"

"You now, food later?"

"Come on, lil daddy," said Meka pulling Face by the hand and leading him to her bedroom.

***

Meka wrapped her hand around the girth of Face's dick and smiled at it as she began to jack him off. She then licked the pre-cum from the head of his dick, swallowed, then wrapped her soft warm lips around the head of his dick.

"Mmmm," Face moaned as he bit his bottom lip and held his hands behind his head. Meka sucked only the head of his dick for a moment, then unexpectedly took all of Face into her throat.

"Ssss, fuck!" He cried as his toes curled.

"Mmmm!" Meka moaned as she bobbed her head slowly, twisting and turning from left to right. Her slow rhythm forced Face to feel all sensitivity of the friction between her mouth and his dick.

"Sssss! Whoo, shit! Damn, you sucking that dick!"

Meka's pussy was drippin' wet from the enjoyment of sucking Face's dick.

"Mmmhmm!" Meka moaned as she massaged his balls and sped up the pace.

Face took his hands from behind his head, gripped her hair with one hand and the sheets with the other.

"Oooouu, eat that dick! Ssss…Fuck yeah!" Face groaned through clenched teeth.

Meka put Face's dick in her mouth until her lips kissed the base of his dick. She held it there for a moment, used her tongue ring to lick the vein on the bottom of his dick, then came up abruptly making a popping sound when snatching the head of his dick out of her mouth. This method caused Face to retreat backwards but to no avail. Meka had a death grip on Face's dick. She had already came twice from sucking Face's dick.

"Ffffuck!" Face's cries could be heard all throughout the house.

Meka continued with her method of madness. She popped the head of Face's dick out of her mouth and cum shot all over her face. Meka jacked Face's dick and slapped it against her face as he continued to skeet on her cheeks, mouth, and nose.

"Damn this old bitch freaky," Face thought to himself as she continued to suck him dry.

Enamored of her freakiness, Face remain aroused. He grabbed her by her hair, pulled her mouth away from his dick, and forced her on her back. Hungry for Face to be deep inside of her, Meka quickly opened her legs widely and licked the cum from her lips. Face was readying himself to enter Meka raw until his mother's words replayed in his mind: *I think I know her. Be careful.*

Face slipped out of bed, retrieved a condom from his pants, then jumped back into the bed. Meka was a bit disappointed but remain appreciative of the young bull's willingness to fuck a woman her age. Eager to have him inside her, Meka grabbed Face's rock-hard dick and guided it to a place where most men lost their minds.

"Mmmm!" Face and Meka moaned in unison as he made his way deep inside of her canal and held it there.

"Damn, this nigga got a condom on, and I still feel the heat from that dick," Meka thought to herself not knowing that Face was thinking the same about her.

Face pulled out of her slowly until the head of his dick was at the entrance of her pussy, then pushed down in her abruptly.

"Hhhhaaa! Yes! Meka moaned.

"Ssshhit!" Face cried as he began to pick up his pace, long stroking her.

"Ssss…Mmmhmmm! Get it!" Meka encouraged as she leaned her head forward and watched as she matched Face's strokes fucking him from the bottom.

Face attempted unpredictable strokes, but Meka was experienced and met him halfway every time.

"Damn this old bitch throwing that pussy," Face thought to himself as he felt an orgasm on the rise.

"Oh, Shit! Sss, oooow, Fffuck!" yelled Face as he turned it all the way up fucking Meka to a violent rhythm.

"Oh, My God! Ssss, Oooooooww…Shit! I'm cuming, baby, Fffuck!" Meka cried as she creamed on Face's dick and shook perpetually.

"Mmmmhmm!" Face moaned, the hairs standing up all over his body as he experienced one of the greatest orgasm he's ever had.

"Damn this pussy good," he whispered, slow stroking her until he was empty.

Face leaned in to kiss her, but she still had his semen on her face. Instead, he pulled out of her and laid beside her, both of them relishing in a euphoric high.

"Wipe yo' face, you still got nut on it."

Meka wiped her face with her shirt and turned her back towards Face.

"Mmmm! Wake me up in thirty minutes," Meka states before going to sleep.

Moments later, Meka was snoring while Face laid parched. He glanced at Meka, then decided to go fetch himself a drink. Face made his way to the kitchen and grabbed a glass of Simply Lemonade. On his way out of the kitchen, he noticed Kiki had made a pallet on the living room floor and was laying on her stomach with one leg arched up. Face made his way over to her, sipped the rest of his drink, then sat the cup on a coffee table, He noted that Kiki had on a T-shirt and some red satin panties, his favorite color. Face took two fingers and rubbed them across her clit causing her to jump a little. She turned around and seen Face standing there.

"Boy, what'chu doing?" Kiki whispered looking around for Meka.

"I told you I got'chu," Face whispered back.

"Where Meka?"

"Sleep. Na boot over and give me some of that pussy," Face demanded slipping his hard dick from his designer briefs.

"Boy you is crazy," Kiki stated while getting on all fours.

Face lifted her T-shirt and pulled her panties to the side.

"Damn," Face whispered amazed at how pretty Kiki ass was.

She was a bit on the fat side, but her ass was well shaped, soft to the touch, smooth and ebony. Face rubbed his dick on her clit for a moment then entered her tight wetness.

"Ssshit!" Face moaned while Kiki did the same with her face buried in a pillow.

He started off with slow steady strokes, while looking back occasionally to see if Meka's door was still closed. After a while he said fuck it and gave Kiki ass all his attention. She had already came the moment Face had entered her, and now her pussy was dripping wet and smacking loudly with even strokes. The sight of Kiki's beautiful, black ass cheeks jiggling amazingly sent Face into animalistic mode causing him to fuck her hard and fast.

Smack! Smack! Smack! Smack! Smack! Smack!

The sounds of Kiki's ass clapping against Face's pelvis echoed loudly throughout the apartment.

"Haaaa... Oooowww, Shit!" Kiki cries managed to escape the pillow.

"Mmmhm!" Face groaned biting his bottom lip.

Face grew longer and harder and began to cum inside of Kiki's good wet, warm pussy.

"Hhhmmmmmm!" Kiki cried in the pillow as she began to squirt all over Face.

Her juices splashed about everywhere while Face continued to pound her from behind until he released all of him. When he snatched out of Kiki, she was still squirting all over her pallet while biting a pillow. Face made his way to the front of her, kissed her on the cheek, then headed back to Meka's room. While in her bed soaked with Kiki's juices on his briefs, he thought of how surprisingly good Kiki's pussy was over Meka's.

Chapter 7
Koko

The next morning Face was awakened by the warmth of Meka's mouth on his dick. When he became fully conscious of what was happening, he couldn't believe that Meka couldn't distinguish the taste between her and Kiki's pussy juice.

"Mmmm!" Face moaned and grabbed a handful of Meka's hair.

Meka moaned and sucked while gazing into Face's eyes loving the reaction she was getting. Right when Meka was attempting to turn it up a notch, her room door opened.

"I cooked break—! Ooouu! I am so sorry," Kiki exclaimed closing the door.

"Damn, bitch! Learn how to knock," yelled Meka attempting to put Face's dick back in her mouth.

"Hold up!" Face asserted pulling away from Meka and hoping out the bed.

"Where you going?" Meka cried.

"I gotta hop in the shower. I got bidness to handle," Face stated grabbing his pants not trusting to leave them with Meka.

"Well, damn, you coulda gave a bitch a quickie! Towels, and rags in there already," Meka motioned disappointedly.

"I'ma be back later, don't trip," Face retorted cutting the water on.

He admired the gold and black décor before hopping in the shower. The steamy water was galvanizing while all kinds of thoughts persuaded his mental. He couldn't believe that he was finally free and had fucked three women less than 48 hours. Face vowed to never love again after April. His heart bore many scars but among them, April's cut the deepest. Face thoughts drifted toward April and stayed there for nearly fifteen minutes. The shower curtain was snatched open interrupting his thoughts.

"You want me to join you?" Meka questioned, smirking mischievously.

"Nah, I was just getting out," lied Face cutting the water off.

Meka frowned and handed Face a towel.

"Breakfast on the table," Meka informed then headed back to the kitchen.

While Face was drying off, his phone rang.

"Yeah?" answered Face without checking the screen.

"I can't believe yo, Face!" Terrell exclaimed hysterically.

"Wassup ma? What'chu tripping on?"

"It's after twelve and you ain't call, came by, or nothin!"

"What'chu talkin about?"

"You said that you was coming by for breakfast! I cooked all this food and you ain't even have the decency to call or nothing!"

"Don't trip ma, I'm finna come grab a plate."

"Don't bother. I threw all that shit away!" *Click!* Terrell hung up the phone pissed way pass pisstivity.

"Damn!" Face pronounced to himself aloud.

He didn't love Terrell, but he appreciated her. Terrell was a good woman... perhaps too good for Face. He was attracted to rachet, furtive bitches, and tended to shy away from the ones you bring home to mama. In Face's mind, why cuff a good woman when he's just gone cheat on her with a slutty rachet one? He finished drying off, wrapped the towel around him and headed to the kitchen. When he entered the kitchen, Kiki couldn't keep her eyes off of Face's well-put-together frame. Her pussy started to throb instantly. Face handed Kiki the keys to his rental.

"Go grab me something from out the back seat to put on," Face ordered casually.

"Okay," Kiki replied excitedly as she made haste to do what she was told.

Meka sat a plate down in front of Face and gazed at him warily.

"Wassup?" Face questioned mixing his corn beef hash together with his cheese eggs and grits.

"Y'all know each other or something?" Meka cantered, envy dripping from her voice.

"N'all, just met her," he retorted blowing his food.

"Well, why the fuck you ain't tell me to go get'chu some shit to wear?"

"You was fixing my food love. Come on nah, you tripping."

"Am I?"

"Come here."

Meka made her way over to Face. He grabbed her and pulled her to his lap.

"Give me kiss," Face requested, poking his lips out.

Meka wasted no time pressing her soft lips against Face's.

"You aight?" He asked rubbing his hands between her thighs.

"I am now."

Kiki came back inside closing the front door behind her.

"I got'cha clothes. You got some nice shit in there! All designer!" Kiki exclaimed impressed.

"Just put it on the couch, I'll get it," Face asserted.

"You finna go?' Meka questioned.

"Yeah, I gotta go handle some shit."

"I need you to do me a favor," Meka remarked.

"Speak on it."

"If I give you the money, will you go bond my daughter out for me?"

"Why you can't do it?"

"I gotta go to Gifford and handle some shit," Meka replied scratching the back of her head as she looked away.

"Yeah this old bitch be trickin'" Face thought to himself. "Yeah, I'll do it. Where she at, Rock Road?" Face inquired.

"Yeah. Here her bond is ten thousand. So, that's a thousand," Meka informed handing face the money.

"Why the fuck Kiki couldn't do it?" Face implored turning his attention towards Kiki.

"I'm going with her," Kiki replied smiling.

Face shook his head.

***

After paying the bondsman, Face pulled up on 23rd and parked in B3's driveway. The bondman said that it would be close to two hours before Meka's daughter's release. Face hopped out, dipped in Maison Margiela from his chest to his shoes. The Cuban on his neck and wrist complimented his panache as he made his way to B3's porch.

"Umm...can I help you?" Ree Ree asked seductively, lusting on what she was seeing.

"Yeah, I'm looking for B3," Face replied. "Tell him Face out here."

"That's my ole man. Give me a minute," Ree Ree shouted before going inside.

Moments later, the girl who came to Face's party with B3 came outside.

"Hey, you remember me? I'm Michelle, B3's sister."

"Yeah, I remember you. How you?"

"Fine, you need anything?" Michelle asked.

"I'm good, thank you."

Ree Ree returned from inside and approached Face.

"B3 in the shower. He told me to tell you don't go nowhere. He'll be right out."

"Aight."

"Boy, you fine as fuck!" Ree Ree admitted brazenly.

Face smile thinking to himself, *"Deez hoes ain't shit!"*

"Hell yeah!" Michelle added.

"Y'all wild as fuck," retorted Face.

"I'm dead ass serious. If B3 wasn't in there, yo' fine ass would be hid up in that muthafucka right na!"

Face just laughed, not sure how to respond to his homie's woman blatant disrespect. The sound of a horn being blown caught Face's attention. The F-350 pulled on the side of the road and a big muscular built figure hopped out. His dredz hung to his stomach with four bust down Cubans the same length. Tattoos littered his face, neck, arms, and legs that told the tales of who he was.

"Face! Wass poppin bloody?"

"Niggaz like us, neva dem! Wass poppin, big homie Kream?" Face greeted, peacing Kream up the way that Bloody Gangstaz do.

"Yo' brother ain't give you the math?"

"Yeah, I got it. I was gone hit'chu fam. I just been enjoying this good pussy out'chere."

"That's understandable! You still supposed to hit me though, blood."

"Why you ain't tell me you brought World home?" questioned Face.

"I really just wanted you to run the G-wall while I take care out here. I ain't want'chu worried about the free world, just make it home. Ya hear me. Yo' brother solid though. He can hold his own, ya hear me."

"I hear you," Face assured.

"Wassup, you need something?" Kream asked going in his pocket and giving Face a stack.

"Bet, though."

"Really, though," Kream replied. "Listen we gotta woop in a couple of days. Make sho you pop out, blood."

"I'm 0-50, my nigga," Face retorted.

"Aight homie. Red Life!" Kream boasted peacing Face before he left.

"The best life! The only life I know!" Face replied.

Kream jumped in his truck and sped off.

"Face! What dey do, mane!" B3 yelled in his Mississippi vernacular.

"Wass popping, my nigga?" Face implored dapping B3 and hugging his neck.

"Boy! You looking good mane!"

"You don't look too bad yourself," Face clowned.

"What'chu finna do, mane?"

"Shid, I come to drink a bottle wit'chu before I go handle some bidness."

"Well, shit mane, where the bottle at?"

Face went to his rental and grabbed a bottle of Casamigos.

"This how we sipping, my nigga. Throw that damn Natural Ice away!"

"Shit, nawl mane," B3 retorted turning the beer can up and finishing it off.

Face just shook his head.

"So you gone talk to Michelle or what mane? She like you, mane," B3 exclaimed.

"I'm good on that," Face cantered.

"Well, shit walk me down here right quick mane," B3 said pointing to his neighbor's apartment.

When they made it to the neighbor's yard, it was a gang of people hanging out. Four sat at a Domino table, while a crowd stood close by politicking.

"You got time to play a few hands?" B3 asked.

"Yeah," Face assured.

"Me and my nigga got next," B3 stated knocking on the table.

49

There were four women present, and Face captured all their attention. The men noted it and hated silently. Face paid them no mind as he popped the bottle and took a shot straight from the bottle.

"Domino!" yelled a little feisty thing slamming the bone down on the table.

"Come on Face, we up," B3 stated taking a seat.

Face hit the bottle then passed it to B3. Face gathered his bones and when it was his turn to play, he knocked on the table.

"You knocking already boo?" flirted the little feisty one.

The tone of her voice and the way that she said it captured Face's attention. He quickly sized her up and noted her black Retro Jordans complimented by an ankle monitor, army fatigue leggings, and a black belly shirt. Her hair was a wavy black fading into light brown pulled back into a long ponytail. She wasn't the prettiest duck in the pond, but her cute round face and succulent lips made her attractive to Face.

"Yeah, I guess I am," Face replied grabbing the bottle from B3.

"Can I hit'cha bottle?" She asked seductively.

"I can't let you hit my bottle if I don't know yo' name," Face flirted back.

"I'm KoKo," she informed with lust in her eyes.

"Wassup KoKo? I'm Face. You can hit my bottle nah that we're no longer strangers.

"Um, I'm go get a cup of ice. Be right back," KoKo retorted then got up to go grab a cup.

When she stood up, Face peeped that she was about 5'6" with a killer stripper body. The arch in her back was raraovis, her walk left all who watched in a luscious state, and her ass cheeks looked to be pillow soft.

"You don't know what to do with that mane," B3 stated smiling knowingly.

"I'm on straight demon time, my nigga," Face remarked.

B3 shook his head up and down laughing. "Aight mane. I tried to tell you."

"Aye B3 we gone," Mario stated as everybody at the table and around it got up to leave.

"Fasho mane, Get at me," said B3 taking a big shot from the bottle and passing it back to Face.

Moments later, KoKo returned with her cup of ice.

"Where everybody went?" She asked.

"I guess they afraid of a lil competition," Face answered.

"Competition for what?" KoKo implied grabbing the bottle and pouring a nice shot.

"Yo' attention," Face cantered smoothly.

KoKo bit her bottom lip seductively.

"You want my attention?" she asked admiring his sexiness.

"I already got it," Face retorted arrogantly.

"Umm…! That you do," KoKo admitted. "How old you is?"

"Twenty-two."

"Ion know bout'chu. I'm four years older than you," KoKo stated.

"I'm grown over here," Face remarked.

"We shall see."

"We shall," Face assured cockily.

"KoKo!" Sugar mama yelled from the apartment.

"Yes, mama?"

"Come start this food, nah!"

"Coming mama!" KoKo yelled back.

"I gotta go handsome," KoKo said standing to leave.

Face grabbed her by her hand stopping her.

"When I'm view you again?"

"You know where I'm at," KoKo replied pointing to her ankle monitor.

Seeing her ankle monitor should have been a warning to Face, but instead it intrigued him.

"Say that then," Face retorted pulling her close.

51

He wrapped his arms around her waist, gripped her ass cheeks, and kissed her tenderly on her neck.

"I'm learn you later," Face uttered backing away slowly.

KoKo bit her bottom lip and gave Face a look that stated, Nigga you don't know who you fuckin with!

Face walked off with B3 and headed back to his whip.

"Boy, KoKo gone take you down through there, mane," B3 warned.

"I'ma hellava nigga 3," Face replied.

"Get at me, mane."

"Love!"

Chapter 8
Yes Sir

Face was in the parking lot of Rock Road county jail waiting for Meka's daughter, Kierra to be released. The Casamigos had him feeling himself as he nodded his head to Lil Polo Da Don's *29 Don*.

How you a street nigga/ holling free a rat/ I couldn't tell on my worst enemy/ I'm built like that/said my name on a post/ Nah that nigga wacked/ can't nobody/not nobody else bring him back/ I'm believe in Jesus/ who I'm praying to all my niggaz in here/ stepping like a band room round of applause/gotta hand it to em yeah you shot me/but yo' nigga dead we ran into em

Face turned the music down when he seen a curvaceous figure 5'5" sashaying towards his vehicle. She had C-cup breast, no stomach, ass and hips for days.

"Damn! That can't be her," Face muttered.

The young woman walked directly to Face's passenger side, opened the door and got in.

"Wassup?" She spoke tenderly.

"Wassup?" Face asked pretending to be appalled. "Who the fuck is you?" Face questioned gripping his pistol.

"Boy, knock it off. My mama already described you and yo' whip," Kierra explained unbothered by his pistol.

"You can never be too careful. I'm just sayin," Face pronounced putting the truck in gear and pulling off.

"You a different type of nigga," Kierra stated.

"I know this."

"You gotta be bringing a gun past them gates," she added eyeing Face.

"Ain't no telling who you might run into lil one," Face declared eyeing her thick thighs.

"My name is Kierra, but you know that already."

Face chuckled as he looked her over. "How old is you?"

"Experienced," Kierra replied as she fooled around with a hanging string of hair in a daintily feminine gesture.

"I'm serious," he declared.

"Me too," Kierra assured seriously. "I'm eighteen."

"Eighteen huh?" Face noticed a tear drop under her left eye.

"What'chu was in for?"

"Damn you all in mines, ana?" Kierra added with a coy giggle.

"Just tryna know who 'round me, lil one," he exclaimed consumed with curiosity.

Kierra gazed at Face thoughtfully before answering.

"I had a gun charge."

"Oh, you in the field like The Children of the Corn, huh?" Face retorted in a tone of reverence.

"You so stupid," Kierra replied tapping Face on his thigh smiling mischievously.

"I took a charge for my nigga," she admitted.

"He kept it solid wit'chu?"

"Fuck no! That nigga lame as fuck," declared Kierra frowning deeply.

"Damn lil one. You a real one. Wish I met'chu before yo' mama."

Kierra glanced at Face barring and infectious smile.

"What'chu shooting yo' shot low key?"

"Just keeping it 5K. For the record, everything I shoot at, I touch." Face cantered tapping his pistol while grinning with an ill suppressed satisfaction.

"Demon-time huh?" she implored turning her body towards him.

This gesture of body language informed Face that she was implicitly comfortable with him.

"You know what's goin on.

"Ummm!" Kierra moaned seductively.

"You hungry, you need something before I drop you off?"

"You know what I need." Kierra stated boldly grabbing a hand full of Face's dick through his Margiela track pants.

"Oooo, I got'chu! I got yo' tough ass," Face assured as his phone rang.

"Yeah, wass poppin'?" Face answered.

Kierra slipped Face's dick from his pants and jacked him off.

"Face! You ain't pick my daughter up yet?" Meka asked, irritation written in her tone.

Kierra eased Face's dick in her warm mouth halfway.

"Shit!" Face cried.

"What happened?" Meka questioned.

"I almost hit a fuckin dog," lied Face.

"You ain't at the jail?"

"I'm headed there, na!"

'Aight, call me when you with her," Meka declared.

"Mmmmhmm!" Face retorted biting his bottom lip

Click! He hung the phone up and enjoyed the head Kierra was giving him.

"Ssss..Shit! Damn! yo' head killing yo' mama's!" cried Face gripping the steering wheel.

For some reason that comment intensified the head that Kierra was giving.

"That's it! Ssss…Fffuck! Get it out of me!" Face coached swerving slightly in another lane.

"Mmmmmm…!" Kierra moaned as her sensitive nipples hardened and her pussy flooded at the very thought of having a real nigga's dick in her mouth.

"That's it! Ssss…Oooou, that's a good girl!

Kierra had her knees in the passenger seat bent over making her ass clap while bobbing her head up and down on Face's dick at a tremendous speed.

"Eat it!" Face encouraged using his right hand to grab a chunk of her plump ass.

No longer being able to control the itch between her thighs, Kierra popped Face's dick out of her mouth.

"Fuck all that shit," Kierra stated removing her Burberry top.

Face was instantly amazed at how perfectly her C-cup breast sat up like two ripe cantaloupes.

"Damn, lil one, relax till we get to a room," Face advised trying to concentrate on the road.

"For what?" Kierra retorted removing her extremely tight Burberry shorts and climbing on top of Face.

"Grab a rubber from the console," said Face.

"Sshh!" Kierra placed her hand over Face's mouth and wiggled down on Face's rock-hard dick.

"Mmmm!" They both moaned in unison.

Kierra removed her hand from his mouth and placed tender juicy kisses on his lips before rising and setting back down on all of him.

"Ffffuck!" Face moaned loving how tight, warm, and wet Kierra's pussy was.

Kierra repeated this motion repeatedly rubbing her titties in Face's face. Her pussy was so good that Face stopped the truck in the middle of traffic on Orange Ave and put it in park. He then lifted the steering wheel, slid his seat back, and grabbed Kierra's ass helping her bounce up and down on his dick at a steady pace.

"Mmmmmhmm! Sss..Yeah! Fuck you thought nigga? I fuck back! Sss...huh? Huh nigga? Sss...yeah! Get it! Ssss...get this pussy!" Kierra taunted through clenched teeth.

Her talking shit turned Face up to the max. He gripped her ass and lifted her off the seat meeting her halfway with devasting thrusts.

"Haaaah, Shit! Ffuck! Sss…Fuck poppa! Alll… Shit,Yesss!" Kierra cried feeling Face in her womb.

"Yeah I know! Killa dick! Take it! Shut the fuck up and take it bitch!" Face vocalized warily.

"Oooooo…pussy skeetin! Oooooooww!" Kierra cried still bouncing wildly on Face's dick.

The sounds of horns could be heard honking, but they paid no mind. Two cars full of teens pulled along aside them with their phones out recording the action.

"Fuck this pussy wet!" Face declared.

"You bet bot nut in this pussy yet, nigga!" Sss…keep that dick hard for this pussy!"

Kierra stopped bouncing on Face and started to grind on him, rolling her back and whining her hips. This method allowed Face to feel all the walls and crevices and cracks within her.

"Oooow, you good pussy bitch," muttered Face.

Kierra began to rock back and forth rapidly.

"This pussy better than my mama's ana? Kierra implored rising to the tip of Face's dick, whining and dropping back down on al of him.

When Face remained silent, silently enjoying the pussy, Kierra started bouncing on Face's dick wildly again.

"Fuck I asked you? Huh nigga?" Kierra asked through clenched teeth.

Face lifted Kierra off of his dick throwing her on the passenger seat on her back. He then grabbed both of her legs and pinned them to the passenger window.

"Oooh shit," Kierra stated, bracing herself for maximum penetration.

Face guided his wet hard dick to her dripping opening and dropped deep off in her.

"Haaaah!" she yelled gripping on anything in the vehicle that was tangible.

"N'all, tough ass nigga!" Face pronounced slamming hard dick in and out of her pussy mercilessly as the trucked rocked back and forth.

"Ssss...oooow! Okaaay!"

"Okay, what nigga?" Face asked through clenched teeth.

"Okaaay.... I feel you poppa!"

"Yeah, I know! Take it!"

"Ooouuw, yes sir! Ssss...yes sir, poppa! Shit, I'm cuming!"

"Paint this dick then! Ssss, fffuck! Paint it, bitch!"

"She paintin' it Poppa, ffffuck!" she cried, squirting all over Face and the interior.

"Damn that pussy squirting!" Face exclaimed.

"And is! Ssss... Oooow God! Yes!"

"That's killa dick! You ever been fucked by a Killa? Huh?" Face implored never missing a beat with his violent strokes.

"Haaaah! Ssss, no Poppa!" cried Kierra.

"Today, yo' day bitch! Ssss..ooou, today yo' fucking day!" Face declared putting everything he had into her.

"Ooooow, pussy skeeting again, Poppa. Whhyy?" Kierra cried as tears of joy fell from her eyes.

Feeling her walls constricting around him, he slowed his pace as she came simultaneously.

"Fuck, Poppa. You gotta bitch crying, that dick so good!" Kierra admitted.

Face pulled outta her and sat back in his seat. He then noticed all the onlookers, put the truck in drive, and pulled off.

"Pussy was crack," Face admitted then his phone rang.

"Yeah?"

"I called; they said Kierra been released. You got her?" Meka asked.

"Yeah, I'm headed to you now."

"Okay, I'm here," Meka retorted. *Click!*
"When we gone rewind that?" Kierra asked.
"You'll know," Face replied dryly.

Chapter 9
V.O.P.

Two days later, Face pulled in front of Koko's mother apartment and hopped out. He noticed B3 down the street, threw his hand up and kept it pushing. Right when he was about to knock on the door, someone opened it.

"Yeah, wassup boi?" asked a familiar face.

Face glanced at the six-foot, one man with familiarity.

"Koko in there?" Face questioned still trying to place the man's face.

"N'all, she went back to the county jail."

"Damn!"

"Yeah, she violated her house arrest," said the familiar face stepping out of the house on the porch.

"Bra, you look familiar as fuck! You played Pop Warner football?" Face implored.

"Yeah! I remember you, boi."

"You played for the Eagles?"

"Yeah!"

"You, G-man?" Face called out.

"That's me. You Face. I told you I remember you," stated G-man.

"How you know KoKo?"

"That's my sister."

"Look I'ma shoot her a kite. Let me get her info and shit."

"Hold up," G-man retorted handing Face a piece of mail with KoKo's name on it.

"Bet, that up," Face proclaimed stuffing the info in his pocket.

"Yeah, yeah. Fuck with me later," G-man pronounced jumping on a bike and riding off.

"Wassup mane?' B3 greeted meeting Face in front of his rental.

"Wass popping?" Face retorted dapping B3 up.

"Heard about KoKo?" asked B3.

"Yeah."

"Aight mane, take heed. That god-damn KoKo a handful mane," B3 informed smirking.

Face phone rang.

"Me too, nigga! Fuck you mean! Yeah, hello?" Face answered.

"You's a real slimy ass, pussy ass, fuck nigga!"

"Who this?" Face asked already knowing who it was. He put it on speakerphone for B3's amusement.

"You know exactly who this is, you nasty trifling bitch!"

"You sound upset. Talk to me," Face clowned.

"You got videos all on Facebook fucking the shit outta my daughter in the middle of the fuckin highway bitch!" Meka spat on the phone.

"I ain't seen it! We went viral?" Face continued to clown.

"Oooow…you's a real pussy nigga!" Meka barked.

"Face you dead ass wrong!" Kiki added.

"Kiki, tell Meka how I fucked the shit out'cha in her living room! Tell her how I had that pussy squirting all over her furniture and carpet!" Face admitted.

"Bitch you fucked him too?" Meka asked with disbelief in her tone.

"Hell yeah! That pussy was good too!" Face added then hung the phone up.

"Mane! You a muthafucka mane! You fuck that woman daughter and her friend mane?" B3 asked smiling.

"Man...! When I was fuckin her daughter, she was somewhere in Gifford tricking! Her and her friend. Them hoez ain't shit fam."

"How old the daughter is?" asked B3.

"She eighteen."

"Pussy good?"

"Pussy crack!" admitted Face.

"Put me in the car," B3 pleaded.

"I got'chu," promised Face.

**

"15, 16, 17, 18, 19, 20!" KoKo counted out her last set of squats.

"Damn bitch yo' ass getting thick! Come here. Let me lick the sweat off that pussy," She She teased grabbing KoKo's ass.

"I might let'chu lick it later," KoKo retorted smiling.

"Bryant!" a C.O, called KoKo for mail.

KoKo left out her cell with a dubious look. She wasn't expecting any mail from nobody. KoKo showed the C.O. her wrist band then grabbed her mail. Once back in her cell, she sat on her rock and couldn't stop smiling at the sender.

"Bitch who wrote 'cho?" questioned She She.

"Somebody I met one day name Face. Damn She She!" KoKo asserted ripping the mail open.

"Face? Blood Face?" she asked.

"I'on know if he a Blood. I met him on the 23rd."

"23rd? Yeah that's his fine ass. I ain't gone cap. I tried to give him this pussy when I was pregnant!" She She stated with no shame.

"Umm mmm!" KoKo said shaking her head.

"Shid, he still can get it!"

KoKo blocked She She out an focused on reading her letter.

KoKo,

Wassup with it Gangsta? I swung thru the 3 to get in yo' chest, but'cha brother informed that you was in the Bing! I'ma pretty said nigga, so I figured I'll check for you in your darkest moment...plus our vibe was genuine the last time we saw each other. I look forward to picking up where we left off. Keep ya head up, ten toes down, two middle fangaz up! Oh yeah, when you get time, check ya account lil baby! Wham Whaz on me! I put a few dollars on the phone too. 772-888-2323.

Respectfully,

Face

P.s I want the first slice of that pound cake when you touchdown! Frfr!

After reading the letter, KoKo couldn't stop smiling. She read it over and over again until she was satisfied.

"Damn bitch! I know you hear me talking to you," She She stated aggravated.

"What?"

"What Face talking about?"

KoKo handed She She the letter then laid back in her rock in a blissful deep thought of Face.

"I got'chu Face," KoKo muttered to herself.

"KoKo!" yelled She She.

"Bitch what?" KoKo yelled back.

"Hoe, you trying to be funny?" asked She She.

"What'chu mean?" KoKo asked confused.

"Bitch, you know I can't read!" She She admitted.

Chapter 10
Bitch Azz Nigga!

*Look it don't matter where I go/ long as my niggaz there
I love my niggaz so much/ can
    follow em anywhere My nigga G-knight yeen gotta worry/
nigga I'ma get us there It hurt
    so much/ to see my nigga on the obituary.*

Face pulled into his mother's yard bumping Lil Polo Da
Don's Long Live G-Knight and spotted his sister and brother
out front smoking a spliff. Before he could put the truck in
park, Sierra made hast to the driver's side of the truck.

"Why the fuck you been ignoring my calls?" Sierra
implored slightly annoyed.

"The tone of yo' voice, it's givin mad, mad. You mad, mad
lil sis? Face clowned his face shaping a smirk.

"You know I gotta take this rental back tomorrow!"

"Calm down, it's gone be aight," Face assured reaching
in his pocket and counting out fifteen hundred dollars.
"Here! Get it for another month and grab you a four for four
at Wendy's or some shit, because you look hungry," Face
continued to clown.

Sierra snatched the money from his hands. "You got me
fucked up nigga! That's where you take yo' lil thots to eat
nigga, nigga. I'm Ruth Criss type bitch! Cheesecake Factory
nigga!" Sierra boated heading to her truck.

World opened the passenger's door and hopped in.

"Wass popping, nigga?" World greeted peacing Face up.

"Us, never them," Face retorted.

"Bra! Why the fuck you playin this clown ass nigga Polo?" questioned World disgusted.

"Fool be sliding! Plus, he the first nigga to make it out the city," defended Face.

"Bra, you know Polo pussy! Heen about none of that shit he be talking about. Plus, he can't even come back to the city.

"That pussy nigga be sliding!" added Face.

World turned the music down. "That bitch ass nigga don't get no play in my shit!" World stated vehemently.

"I'm done rapping 'bout that clown. On some other shit though, the big homie Kream caught an attempted murda in the state, plus an indictment from the Fedz on some dope shit."

"Damn! Hopefully, the homie will come from up under that," Face retorted optimistically.

He then counted his money and noted that he was down to fifteen hundred dollars.

"Damn, my shit getting low," cried Face.

"Shid, what'chu wanna do?" asked World.

Before Face could consider an option, his phone rang.

"Yeah!"

"Thank you for using Global Tel-link. You have a pre-paid call from KoKo press—"

Face accepted the call.

"Wassup with it, Gangsta?" Face greeted.

"Oh my God! Face heyyy!" KoKo responded with obvious excitement in her voice.

"You sound happy to be talking with me? You miss me?"

"Maybe."

"Maybe? I can feel you smiling through the phone from ear to ear."

"Well, you the only one who been here for me, so I am feeling some type of way about'chu," KoKo admitted.

"You feelin a way 'bout a nigga huh?"

"I am," she assured feeling like a young teenage girl again.

"So, what we gon' do about that?"

"I'on know, Face. You ain't ready, you are still fresh out. You might wanna roam around a lil more before playing in this pond," KoKo warned.

Face laughed undauntedly. "When you touch down?"

"I gotta court date coming up in a few weeks. Hopefully, I'll get out then."

"I'm waiting on you."

"You want this pound cake, huh?" KoKo implored seductively.

"You know what time it is."

"I hear you daddy," she exclaimed with a light chuckle.

"What'cha books lookin' like? You good?"

"Yeah, I'm good. Thank you, like for real, Face."

"No pressure."

"Listen, they lockin' down, so I'ma call you some other time. I want'chu to think hard about what I said."

"Ain't nothing to think about," Face assured.

"Aight, talk to you later.

"Yeah!" *Click!*

Face hung the phone up smiling.

"Who that?" World questioned.

"This older baby I ran across. She locked up right na, but she about to come home."

World shook his head. "Pay attention to the signs, fool. Why you fuckin with bitches in jail?"

"I met her before she went in. I ain't tryna marry the hoe. I just wanna see what that top and bottom do when she jump," Face proclaimed.

"I can view it na! I bet'chu she brazy as fuck!" World warned.

"Dem brazy bitches be having the best pussy," Face cantered thinking with his little head.

"You love that toxic shit. That shit gone be yo' downfall bra," World informed concerned.

Moments later, Face's phone rang again.

"Yeah?" he answered.

"Wassup, sextape?"

"Who this?"

"This Kierra!"

"Ohh shit! What dey do porn star?" Face clowned.

"I'm Gucci," she replied jubilantly.

"You know after we went viral, yo' mama called me snapping," Face said laughing.

"Yeah I know. We got into it and shit, but I had to tell her like you done fucked one of my niggas, so we even bitch," Kierra proclaimed.

"You good though?"

"Yeah, me and my mama gotta bond that can't be broken. We fight and make up all the time. But yeah man that video got so many niggas in my inbox it's krazy! That's part of the reason I'm calling you."

"Talk to me," Face retorted.

"I got one for us, if you with it," Kierra offered.

"Say none. I'm pulling up on ya na."

"I'm sending yo' the addy na," she said.

"Yeah!" *Click!*

"I got one for us, bra."

"You know what it is with me," World stated arrogantly.

***

I'ma real top shotta/ I got some niggaz who'll cross yo' ass out like Mufasa/ We'll do whatever for the dollarz...Bitch! Yeah...We'll do whatever for dollarz! /
I might be da nigga who robbed ya/
I might know who shot ya partna/
I might be all in ya crib/
Wit dick all in ya bitch stomach/ all in her ribs/

Turn ya head to beef tips/ turn ya chest to beef strips/

The sound of 210 Slick's Top Shottaz saturated the minds of World and Face readying them for a drill that could possibly turn deadly. World was sipping Patron on ice, while Face was taking bumps of clean coke. He acquired this habit at the age of thirteen when he lost his cousin Stacey to gunfire on Christmas morning. This choice of drug earned him the name Face. World turned the music down before speaking.

"Bra, who this nigga is? He Fie!" implored World.

"That's my nigga from Perry, Florida, 210 Slick. I met 'em in prison. He a real one, and he about his issue," Face stamped.

"I'ma have to see what else he hollin' 'bout."

Face looked at the time and seen that it was 10:35 p.m.

"Damn! She say she was gone text me at ten to let me know she was gone and the nigga in there," Face pronounced.

"Shid, give her 30 more minutes. If she don't hit by then, fuck it, we goin in," World exclaimed.

"Bet," Face agreed taking another one-on-one to the nose.

World looked at Face concerned.

"Bra, be careful who you get'cha coke from. Bitches been dying left and right. These niggas cutting that shit wit Fent bra."

"I know bra, I got a solid plug tho. I'm good," Face assured.

Thirty minutes passed and still no call from Kierra.

"Fuck it bra, we in there," Face ordered hopping out of the truck with World behind him,

The spot was secluded on a dirt road with no lights and almost no neighbors. When making their way to the trap, Face glanced behind him and spotted a fiend approaching.

"Hold up bra," whispered Face slowing down so the fiend could catch up.

World surveyed their surroundings while waiting.

"Wassup unk? What'chu need? Face questioned.

"N'all nephew, I'm good. I'm headed right there to Oonk's spot, exclaimed the fiend who was dressed in a dirty FUBU outfit.

"Hold up unk. You wanna make fifty dollars?"

"Hell, shit, yeah! What'chu need unk to do, baby? He asked scratching his chest.

"Just knock on Oonk's door for me and the money yours," Face promised.

"That's it?"

"Yeah," said Face.

"Unk got'cha," the fiend assured eagerly leading the way.

Face crept up from the left side of the house, World made his way from the right, and the fiend walked straight up the driveway passing a sky-blue CTS sitting on 22's. Face drew his DVG-1 9mm, and World already had his Glock-22 out. The fiend didn't even pay attention to their apparent movement. He just wanted the fifty dollars. He knocked on the door, then continued to scratch his chest as he waited. Moments later, the door opened.

"What'chu want Unk? You, still—"

Oonk noticed something out of his peripheral and tried to close the door out of pure instinct, but Face sticking his Glock in the door canceled that.

Boc! Boc!

Face let off two shots hitting Oonk in the jaw. Oonk took off running, holding his face while Face gave chase. World grabbed the fiend, forced him inside and locked the door behind him.

Boc!

World put one in the fiend's top then followed behind Face. When Face made his way into the room that Oonk ran in, he spotted Oonk holding Kierra in front of him as a shield.

"You's a real bitch ass nigga!" expressed Face.

"Where it at!" screamed World, his Glock trained on the duo.

Kierra was startled but kept her composure.

"Ain't nothing here man," cried Oonk who was crying real tears while blood poured from his wound.

"Nigga get the fuck off me and tell dem niggaz where that shit at!" Kierra exclaimed seething.

The sight of his intruders wearing latex gloves and no mask terrified Oonk. He knew the chances of living after telling them where the stash was, was slim to none.

"Where the fuck it at?" Face implored in a dangerously calm tone.

"I'm tellin' you, it ain't nothin here," Oonk pleaded tears and blood falling from his face simultaneously.

"Let her go nigga," Face demanded through clenched teeth.

Oonk let Kierra go and raised his hand in the air.

"Don't kill me, my nigga! If it was here, I woulda been gave it up! I'on want to die 'bout this shit!"

Face placed the top of his pistol on the bridge of Oonk's nose.

"Wea it at?"

"Ain't nothin…" *Boc!*

Face hit Oonk right between the nose, splatting brain fragments and blood all over Kierra's face before dropping lifeless. Kierra closed her eyes and wiped what she could from her face.

"Why the fuck you ain't text me?" Face questioned.

"This nigga took my phone and wouldn't let me leave," Kierra retorted.

"Maan…! Fuck all that! Wea it at, bitch!" World enunciated agitated and pointing his Glock in her face.

"It's a book bag in the closet, in the hallway. That's all I know man," Kierra states firmly.

Face took off to go investigate. World went through Oonk's pocket and removed a small knot that was only twenty-eight hundred. Face found the book bag and found just two pounds of loud.

"Who, you gone tell?" World questioned Kierra; his pistol aimed at her.

"Nobody man! I'on even know this nigga!"

World smiled. "I know you ain't bitch." *Boc!*

He hit Kierra in the head dropping her. Face made his way back to the room.

"Damn, bra you killed the hoe?" Face asked slightly disappointed.

"Bitch seen our face nigga!" World retorted and left the room.

Face gazed at Kierra for a moment. He actually liked Kierra and her energy. Moments later, World came back in the room with a knife. He squatted, lifted Kierra's head up and slid the knife across it. Face shook his head but will never put nothing before his brother.

"Come on nigga!" World screamed pulling on Face's shirt.

Face glanced at Kierra once more before taking off behind World.

Chapter 11
Rock Solid

Three days later, Face pulled up on B3 with a bottle of Remy and a few blunts of Za. After only walking away from the lick with fourteen hundred, a pound of Za, and a dead friend, he needed to unwind. Smoke bled from his nose as he thought of Kierra.

"Wassup mane?" B3 questioned after coming from his room.

"Vibin," Face retorted passing the blunt to B3.

"I was back there reading this shit mane. These muthafuckaz round here vicious mane." B3 exclaimed passing a newspaper to Face.

Face hit the Remy out the bottle, sat it down, then grabbed the newspaper. Clear as day the headliner read in big black bold letters…

GRUESOME ROBBERY LEAVES MAN DEAD AND A WOMAN HOSPITALIZED!

Face glanced at B3 then back at the paper.

"Yeah that shit wild! Somebody shot the girl and cut her throat!" Face added loudly, but silently thought to himself, *how could Kierra still be alive, and would she tell?"*

He handed the paper back to B3 and took another sip from the bottle. B3 had the paper close to his face.

"Damn mane! This girl look just like the one from that video you went viral with. The one you was fucking on camera!"

"Let me view that," Face asked playing it cool, already knowing who it was.

Face studied the picture of Kierra.

"Damn, that is her!" Face remarked dramatically.

"Somebody tried to kill ya bitch, mane" said B3.

Seconds later, a pretty young thang walked through B3's front door changing all train of though. She was slim-thick, almond colored skin with resemblance of Keke Palmer.

"Damn! Who the fuck is that?" Face questioned.

"You can't do nothin with that. That's KoKo lil sister," B3 informed smiling. "You can't have both mane. Wassup CC?"

"Hey B3," CC replied standing directly in front of Face presenting one of the prettiest camel toes Face had seen since being free.

CC had on tight pink nylon leggings, a black belly shirt, and some pink and black Asics.

"Who you is boy?" CC asked locking her legs with her hands on her curvy hips.

"If you don't know me, you can't be from the city. Either you ain't from the city, or you just to young to know," Face expressed taking another shot of Remy.

"Boy, I'm from right here, and I'm eighteen," she replied voice soft as snow.

"I'll be back mane. I gotta shit bad as hell," B3 announced holding his stomach before walking off.

"So, wassup with'chu? You talk to my sister?" CC implored.

"Yeah, we talk, but I ain't fuck her of nothing."

"You know she violated her house arrest for leaving to go see a nigga," CC informed.

Instead of taking heed to what CC was saying about her older sister, Face took it as haterism, making him want KoKo more.

"Wassup wit'chu?" Face asked rising from B3's couch and circling CC like a hungry vulture.

"What'chu want to be up?" she retorted.

Face grabbed a hand full of CC's ass.

"Damn, that ass soft,"

Face then grabbed a hand full of her pussy. His dick immediately turned rock solid.

"Damn! That pussy warm and fat as fuck! Come on, let's slide in that bathroom right there," Face advised biting his bottom lip and grabbing his dick.

"Mmm, mmm! You ain't finna just fuck me in no bathroom like a lil hoe. You want this pussy; nigga get a room."

Face contemplated her request digging in his pocket. When digging in his pocket he thought about the lick he'd just hit and how he should warn his brother about Kierra's survival. Then he thought about KoKo. He knew if he fucked KoKo little sister that shit would be different.

"Look as bad as I wanna take yo' lil sexy ass down, I'ma have to catch you another time ma," Face mentioned regretfully.

"Yo loss," CC replied arrogantly.

Face grabbed his bottle of Remy.

"You good in here, mane?" B3 asked coming from the back of his apartment.

"I'ma catch you later fam," Face told B3 dapping him up.

"Yo homeboy trippin," said CC lusting on Face.

His babyface full of ink, his neck and wrist drippin, and attire had CC's pussy wet as a Manta Ray.

"I told you, I'ma catch you," Face assured walking out of B3's apartment. B3 laughed and smiled at CC.

"What happened?"

***

When Face entered Kierra's room, a young beautiful nurse was sitting a tray of blended food in front of her. Even though World failed indubitably at slitting Kierra's throat, unfortunately she still had to sip her meals through a straw.

"If you need anything, just give me a ring," said the nurse.

When the nurse turned to leave, Kierra spotted Face standing with a plaintive expression.

"Hi," the nurse uttered before leaving the room.

"Face?" Kierra asked in a tone of feigned surprise.

Face made his way to the side of her bed, her eyes trained on him all the while.

"Before you zap out on me, I came to apologize for my brother. I shuda never left the room and I take full responsibility. I didn't think you was in the house, and I forgot to express to him that you was off limits."

"Ssshh! Boy, I ain't gone say nothing. Even though yo' brother was dead ass wrong, I ain't no police ass bitch. Just keep yo' brother the fuck away from me. Can't even slit a bitch throat right," Kierra expressed her face shaping a mischievous smirk.

Face chuckled before speaking. He found her perspective riveting.

"Damn, you real as fuck! I'm forever indebted to you. You ever need anything just say that and it's done. ANYTHANG!" assured Face.

Even though Kierra's head and neck were bandaged up, she still chortled.

"You already know what I want," she retorted grabbing a handful of Face's dick. "As soon as they relieve me, come drop it off." She stated winking her eye.

Face smiled shaking his head in adulation.

"You know I got'chu," Face exclaimed.

***

Face left the hospital elated that Kierra was rock solid. He pulled into his mother's driveway on Avenue S bumping 210 Slick...

Lord please help me out/deez niggaz snitching/workin wit wires/ I guess they all some electricians/ workin wit wires/ and the Fedz to get me a sentence/ You know they wanna see me/ Spend my whole life in prison/ Trying to lock me up foreva/ Say I influence niggaz/ everytime it pop off/ they swear I know who the shooter is/ All my residents/ Searching for evidence/ You ain't gotta search warrant kraka/ what'chu find is irrelevant/

The loud music brought World outside. He made his way to Face's rental and hopped in the passenger's seat. Face turned the music down.

"Wass popping?" Face greeted.

"Niggaz like us," World retorted bumping Bs with Face.

"You see the papers?" questioned Face.

"N'all, wassup wit it?"

"The nigga, Oonk dead, but Kierra still alive," Face informed.

"Shid…you know the protocol! Let's go get her!" World exclaimed diabolically.

"Relax homie. I already pulled up, and barked with her. We good." Face assured.

"Man, fuck all that! I ain't taking no chances," World pronounced.

"If she was gone put us in the blender, dem Krakaz woulda been scrapped us off the streets. She know where we at. Kierra ain't no police ass bitch. She solid, bra."

World looked at Face ambivalently.

"Aight nah!" World warned.

Chapter 12
Mixed Feelings

Two weeks later...

Face was sitting in B3's living room smoking a blunt with Chelle. Chelle was the girl that B3 had tried to put on Face at his welcome home party. She stayed across the street from B3. Face noted Chelle's sultriness but played it with nonchalance. As thick and soft as her perfectly shaped ass was, he didn't want to open them doors. Face thought it better to remain friends.

"Yeah bra, I'll be off this house arrest shit in a few weeks. We gone make some shit happen!" Robert exclaimed.

"I'm wit'chu," Face retorted passing Chelle back the blunt.

"Maaan! You ain't been fucking with a nigga! I ain't seen you since yo' welcome home party nigga!"

"I been trying to formulate some motion, plus I ain't trying to be at yo' spot with pistols and shit on me. Them Krakaz monitoring you, nigga," explained Face.

Robert laughed. "Stop being scary, nigga!"

Face chuckled before replying. "Nigga you know my work," Face stated arrogantly.

"You know I'm just fuckin wit'chu my dog," Robert assured. "I'ma fuck wit'chu doe, my nigga," Robert assured hanging up.

Chelle took another toke from the blunt, then passed it back to Face.

"If you hungry, Face, I cooked a pot of greens, fried chicken, and mac-n-cheese," Chelle offered.

"I'm good Chelle but thank you though."

"Okay, but'chu don't know what'chu missing," Chelle retorted seductively.

Seconds later, B3 entered through the front door apprehensively.

"Boy! KoKo out, boy!" B3 announced excitedly.

Chelle's whole attitude changed. She was one of many women who despised KoKo.

"Nigga stop lying," Face retorted not believing him.

For real mane!"

Moments later, KoKo entered B3's apartment looking emotionally depleted. Her hair was frizzy, her skin a little lighter than before, and she had on a McDonald's uniform that she had apparently got arrested in. When she spotted Face, she became self-conscious and used her right palm to pat her loose hair. Face stood up and closed the space between them.

"Damn, wassup?" implored Face wrapping his arms around her stripper frame.

"Heeyy, Face," KoKo replied cutting the hug short.

Chelle got up and made an exit dripping exasperation.

"You don't seem too elated to see me."

"N'all, it ain't that. I'm just ready to get this jailhouse stench off me," she explained giving herself a once over.

"That's understandable. Let me walk you home."

KoKo turned to leave with Face close behind.

"Why you ain't call me, and tell me you was getting out?"

"I didn't even know. They woke me up for court this morning and the judge gave me time served," she exclaimed.

Face noted her provocative strut and apparently others did too.

"Koko, wassup? I see you back out here. You wanna get a bottle?" said some nigga in a Toyota.

"N'all I'm good," Koko assured brushing him off and keeping it pushing.

Instead of Face seeing this as a sign of her being a thot, he took it as her being most wanted.

"Damn this bitch sexy as fuck." Face thought silently.

"So wassup?" You wanna grab something to eat and get a room?" Face offered when they reached her mother's porch.

"Ummm...my Mama wanted me to stay home tonight, plus she already cooked for me so..."

"Shid, ask her if you can have some company tonight," Face quipped as he ambled towards her and wrapped his arms around her.

He gazed in her eyes and gripped both of her pillow soft ass cheeks, KoKo arched her back slightly as she took a deep breath and contemplated the thought.

"I'on think Suga Mama gone go for that one," KoKo replied calling her mother by her nickname.

Face grinned.

"Suga Mama, huh?" He chuckled. "Just ask her."

"Okay. Give me a minute," KoKo pronounced as she turned to go do as she was told.

When KoKo entered the apartment, her little sister CC was coming out.

"Damn," Face whispered as he noted her meaty camel toe and flat stomach.

CC had on a black crop top, some black booty shorts, and a pair of black and pink Pumas. With no regard for her sister or the nigga waiting parked on the side of the road, CC stepped right in front of Face eyeing him from head to toe.

"Hey Face."

"Wassup with it?"

"Damn, red look good on you," she complimented Face's Bally get down.

"I know this," he retorted arrogantly.

CC smiled unyieldingly. The sound of a horn being blown broke their gazes.

"You better slide fo' homie fuck you up," Face teased.

"Tss…whateva," CC replied then walked away her ass jiggling elegantly all the way to the vehicle that awaited her.

Moments later, KoKo strutted outside her face shaping a felicitous smile.

"What'chu smiling bout gorgeous?"

"My mama said yeah," KoKo informed in disbelief.

***

Face was laid comfortably naked in KoKo's bed when she entered the room fresh out of the shower in a blue and black night gown that sat right above her camel toe.

"Damn," Face mumbled under his breath.

"You alright in here?" KoKo implored with a sexy saunter towards her vanity.

"Hell yeah," Face quipped his voice dripping nostalgia.

KoKo smiled, lit a scented candle and turned on Rome's *Do You Like This*. The salving sounds serenated the room. KoKo crawled provocatively into the bed and placed a tender kiss on Face's foot. She then gazed into his eyes as she took a few of his toes into her mouth and sucked them gently.

"Da fuck," Face moaned jumping a little from the extreme warmth of her mouth. He had never had his toes sucked before, but the feeling was blissful.

"Mmm," KoKo moaned, massaging his foot while sucking and licking his toes.

"Damn this bitch a cold animal," Face confirmed in his mental

She made her way to his ankles and began to place a trail of soft wet kisses up his leg. KoKo grabbed his dick that was hard as granite and was impressed with the length and girth.

"Mmm," she moaned from the electricity that shot through her pussy.

The foreplay that she was administering had her pussy extremely wet. She kissed and sucked in between Face's thighs while jacking his dick slowly.

"Fffuck…" Face cried jumping and shaking from her abstruse touch.

The sensation that he was experiencing was foreign. It gave him mixed feelings, although most blissful. He also felt confounded. A woman had never tended to his anatomy with such care and passion. KoKo moved from Face's thighs to his balls sucking them as she continued to jack his dick.

"Shhit!" Face cried, gripping the coco butter scented sheets.

She removed her mouth from his balls, used her right hand to massage them, and placed the head of his dick in her mouth.

"Mmm.." Koko moaned as she tasted and swallowed his pre-cum.

After tampering with the head of his dick, she unexpectedly slid the majority of Face's shaft into her warm mouth.

"Umm-huh!" Face shriveled biting his bottom lip.

KoKo bobbed her head slowly from the tip to the base of Face's dick while massaging his shaft and twisting her head from right to left artistically.

"Damn, you sucking that dick," Face whimpered as his legs began to tremble in pleasure.

With no warning KoKo impetuously advanced the motion of her head slurping and sucking with purpose.

"Oh…fffuck!" Face cried as he came in KoKo's mouth gripping the sheets for dear life.

KoKo swallowed every drop with breathless moans and continued to suck Face's dick deliriously forcing him to stay hard. After draining every specimen, she straddled Face's lap and placed a trail of kisses from his neck to chest. She kissed and sucked his nipples hungrily, grabbed his dick and rubbed it against her swelling clit. It grew more sensitive with every stroke. Gasping as she lowered herself, his large dick head pressed against her g-spot before settling deep inside her. They both moaned, her tight wet warmth gloving him as his size stretched her deliciously. She place her hands on his chest and gazed in his eyes biting her bottom lip as she began to ride him slow and sufficiently.

"Ssss…ooow, this pussy good," Face moaned as his hands caressed her back sliding lower to massage and squeeze he soft rotund ass cheeks. He grabbed them both and thrusted upward to a rhythm that was in sync with her movement.

"Ssss, whooo, daddy this dick good," KoKo cried as she sped up her motion winding and bouncing chaotically like a nymphomaniac contortionist.

"Fffffuck! Sss, that's it! Put that pussy on me! Sss… ooo sshit!" Face moaned.

KoKo's pussy was so good that Face had to reframe himself from telling her he loved her.

"Oooow, daddy, pussy skeeting," KoKo cried out as her sodden pussy creamed all over his dick.

Her walls constricting around his shaft forced him to cum seconds after her. The warmth from his semen was pleasing to her insides. KoKo was astonished to find Face still erect. Normally, her partners were weak and unable to perform after coming once. His stamina turned her on. She hopped off Face's dick and buried it in her mouth repeatedly. Face talked dirty through clenched teeth while KoKo moaned, slurped, and sucked until the throb deep in her pussy was too much to bear. After pulling Face's dick from her mouth, she mounted him reverse cowgirl and bounced up down while rubbing her clit.

"Ooow, daddy!"

"Ride that dick," Face encouraged loving her performance.

KoKo's ass cheeks jiggled egregiously as she continued to manipulate her clit and pinch her left nipple while bouncing wildly.

"Ssss...ooow...suwoo! Sss...Suwoo!" KoKo cried switching her motion from bouncing to hard grinding gyration.

She knew that Suwoop was a Blood lingo and wanted Face to know that she knew who he was.

"Bdddattt!" Face retorted as he felt KoKo constrict and cream all over him.

Her pussy was gushing, and Face could feel her wetness in his lap. KoKo hopped off of his dick and cleaned it with her mouth, moaning excessively. KoKo's head was so phenomenal that Face had to stop her, grab her by the throat and kiss her passionately. He then broke away from the kiss to speak his mind.

"Damn, you eat that dick the greatest," he admitted.

KoKo snuffled a sexy chuckle displaying a furtive grin. Face grabbed her and guided her on her back. He removed her nightgown, parted her legs and began to massage her thighs while kissing them tenderly. Moving towards her inner thigh, he noted a birthmark that was shaped like a peach and found it remarkable. He kissed and massaged it.

"Damn this bitch thighs soft as fuck." Face thought to himself.

When he became face to face with her passion fruit, he was in awe. It was the fattest, prettiest pussy he'd ever encountered. His mouth watered before placing a kiss on her clit.

"Sss...umm!" KoKo shivered and jumped from the soft touch of Face's lips.

He placed his palms in the back of her knees and pent her knees to her midsection. Right when KoKo braced herself for what's to come, Face latched on her clit. He flicked his tongue rapidly, sucked and blew gently forcing KoKo to gasp, whimper, and yelp while gripping the sheets. Face moaned while eating KoKo's pussy performing the lick, suck, and blow ritual until she grabbed the back of his head and fell into an epileptic state.

"Whooo...daddy...Pussy skee...sss...pussy skeeting," she cried winding her pussy in his face.

"Umm," Face moaned as he swallowed everything her pussy dripped.

After eating her pussy, he wanted her to taste her own juices. He crawled up her cotton soft body leaving a trail of kisses behind until he reached her bibulous lip. Face kissed her proficiently and slid his pulsating dick into her warm, wet canal.

"Hmmm," KoKo cried her knees trembling as he slid in slow and deep.

"Ffffuck," Face added as he started on a steady pace.

He placed one of her nipples in his mouth and sucked while grinding in and out of her.

Sss, ssshit!" Face moaned snatching out of her trying not to come prematurely.

"What daddy?" KoKo implored.

"Pussy good," Face admitted rubbing his dick on her clit before pushing back down in her.

"Ooow!" KoKo moaned.

Face placed her left leg up over his right shoulder, got into a push-up position then commenced to stroke her ferociously.

"Oooow, you deep! Sss...Whoo, daddy you deep!" KoKo confessed both of her arms placed behind her head gripping a pillow as she watched Face's wet thick, long dick po-go in and out of her dripping pussy.

"Ssss...ooow...You good pussy bitch! Ssss...ffffuck! I'm finna nut all in this good pussy," Face cried through clenched teeth while noting how rapidly her titties were bouncing with each stroke.

"Nut in this pussy! Sss...oow, yesss, nut all in this fat pussy daddy!"

"Ssss,oooooooww sssshit, I'm skeeting in this pussy!" Face growled throwing his dick fast and hard trying to throw his back out.

KoKo felt Face's warm semen shoot deep within her. "Whoo, daddy! I feel you! Ssss…ooow,pussy skeeting daddy, fffuck!" KoKo cried as her legs began to shake uncontrollably.

Once her orgasm began to subside, she leaned forward and placed kisses on Face's chest. He reciprocated by placing kisses on her cheek, neck, and forehead. KoKo slowly turned Face over and lowered herself, putting Face's dick in her mouth. She moaned as she cleaned their bodily fluids from his dick. Face laid back biting his bottom lip with his eyes closed. The after effect from his orgasm felt like a shot of morphine. KoKo was so fixated on keeping Face's dick in her mouth that he had to pull her mouth off his dick. He pulled her up and wrapped her in his arms. KoKo kissed Face on his neck then laid her head on his chest. Within seconds later, Face fell into a deep sleep.

"Face! Daddy, wake up," Koko muttered shaking Face awake.

When Face's vision cleared, KoKo was standing next to the bed with a plate and a glass cup.

"Wassup, ma?" he implored sitting up in the bed.

"Here, daddy. I made you a BLT and some Kool-Aid," KoKo stated handing Face the plate and sitting the cup on the nightstand.

The bacon, lettuce, and tomato sandwich smelled delightful. He took a bite, closed his eyes and savored the flavors popping all over his tongue. When he opened his eyes, KoKo was massaging his feet proficiently.

"You, like it, daddy?" KoKo asked.

"Damn my nigga, I think I love this hoe already." Face thought to himself.

85

Chapter 13
Don't Do It

The next morning Face was awoken by a delectable stench and incredibly warm sensation between his knees. When his vision became vivid, he became aware that the warm sensation was KoKo's mouth. She gazed into his eyes undaunted as she did what she did best.

"Ffffuck," Face moaned grabbing a handful of her wavy hair.

Noting that he was fully awake, KoKo applied pressure moaning, sucking, and slurping rigorously while playing with her clit. Withing minutes, KoKo had forced Face to cum in her mouth. She swallowed every drop while cuming herself.

"Ummm…good morning daddy."

"Ssshit! Morning, sexy," Face retorted galvanized.

KoKo got up walked to the nightstand, grabbed a plate and handed it to Face.

"This cheese egg and bacon sandwich, and a glass of Simply Mango. When you finish eating, get dressed. Mama say it's time for company to leave. She say she heard us last night too," KoKo pronounced smiling.

"That was yo' ass," Face stated biting his sandwich.

"Boy that was both of us," KoKo replied walking towards the door.

"I'm finna go brush my teeth. Be ready when I get back," she exclaimed leaving the room.

Face looked at her thoughtfully as she left the room. *"Dam...good pussy... fie head... a nice vibe and this bitch can cook? She don't own a car or home, but shid we can change that."* Face mulled to himself.

He finished his food then got dressed. Instead of waiting on KoKo to finish in the bathroom, Face made his way to the living room where KoKo's mother was seated watching TV. Face approached her and held out his hand.

"Good morning, Sugar Mama," Face greeted.

Sugar Mama held out her hand and Face grabbed it placing a tender kiss on it.

"Umm-huh! Good morning to you too," she retorted with a smirk on her face.

"Damn she sexy," Face thought to himself.

Face went in his pocket and pulled out a small knot.

"I owe you for the hospitality," he states handing her a few bills.

"Boy, put'cho money in ya pocket and make yo' way out that door," Suga Mama retorted secretly admiring him,

"Yes ma'am," Face said before leaving.

When Face made it outside he noted that it was smoggy. He walked across the small lawn, made his way to the end of the driveway and posted on the curb. After ponderous moments of KoKo's performance ticked by, Face was startled by a familiar voice.

"Boy I see you just left KoKo house. What' chu was in there getting fie brain? A youngin by the name of Suavey implored with a knowingly grin plastered across his face.

Suavey's presence and remark caught Face off guard, but he played it cool. Face used to run the streets with Suavey's older brother before he caught a lengthy bid.

"You, already know," Face retorted dapping Suavey up.

"How the fuck this lil nigga know KoKo gotta mean head game?" Face thought.

"That's real my nigga! I'm fuck wit'chu," Suavey added before walking off.

Moments later, Face felt arms wrapping around his waist. He turned around and looked KoKo in her dreamy eyes.

"Damn, what'chu was in there shitting?" he clowned.

KoKo laughed before replying. "No, silly. I had to clean this pussy."

"That's a whole lotta cleaning," Face exclaimed grabbing a handful of pussy.

"What'chu trying to say? My pussy smell?"

Koko knocked his hand away.

"N'all...that pussy big and good," Face admitted.

"My pussy in not big, it's just fat."

"And good," Face added.

KoKo chuckled sexily biting her bottom lip. "What'chu finna get into?" she questioned.

"I'm finna head cross town to handle something. Walk me to my truck," Face exclaimed motioning his head to his rental that was parked in B3's yard.

KoKo sauntered alongside Face with a vivacious smile.

"What'chu smiling about?" Face implored studying her face.

KoKo shrugged her shoulders. "I'on know. I guess because you got me feelin like a new woman," she declared stopping next to Face's rental.

"Oh, yeah?"

"Umm-huh," KoKo assured wrapping her arms around Face's neck and placing a tender kiss on his lips.

Face obliged gripping her extra soft ass cheeks.

"Damn, that ass soft. Umm!" Face expressed sucking on her bottom lip.

"It's all yours, daddy."

"Boy, I see you boy!" B3 yelled from his porch.

Face nodded his head at B3 then averted his attention back to KoKo.

"Who truck is this?" she questioned.

"It's a rental."

"You coming back?"

"Yeah, I'ma be back though. You need something?"

"No, I'm good. Just make sho' you come back," KoKo stated kissing Face and turning to leave.

Face watched her walk away loving every second of it until a car horn broke his trance. When Face turned to see who it was, he recognized the driver. It was an old head he knew from being in the streets. Face walked in the street and stood next to the driver's side.

"Buger Bear! Wassup O.G.?" Face greeted dapping him up.

"Face! You back out here, huh?

"Been out, a few weeks nah," Face informed.

"Glad to see you back out here. Listen, hop in for a minute. Let me bark at'chu."

Face looked back at B3 then turned and headed to the passenger side. He got in and Buger Bear pulled off.

"How long you been gone, lil homie?"

"Two years."

"You know who that is that you was just hugged up with?" Bear asked occasionally glancing at Face then back at the road in front of him.

"KoKo? Yeah, I just met her," Face declared feeling uneasy about the question.

Buger Bear shook his head in disdain. "Don't do it, lil homie. You, a lil real nigga. Tru playa and I'on wanna see you go out like that."

"Like what?" Face questioned perplexed.

"How old you is?"

"Twenty-two."

"Yeah, she a lil older than you. Listen, KoKo been off the porch to fuck with this dope boy from the bottom and they say he sick."

"Sick?" Face implored.

Buger nodded.

"Damn, I just hit this hoe raw dog," Face thought to himself.

"Good looking out, O.G.," Face exclaimed dapping Bear up as they pulled back in the front of B3's apartment.

"Aight, lil homie. Be safe. You know how these niggas is out'chere.

"It's been a lot of killing lately."

"I keep it on me," Face assured flashing his pistol. "But good looking out," said Face hopping out of Bear's Crown Victoria.

Buger Bear blew the horn then pulled off. B3 stepped off his porch and made his way to Face.

"Wass good mane? I see you stayed down there to KoKo's all night," B3 asserted, smiling gleefully.

"Bra, you some shit!" Face declared, his face leathered and creased.

"How you mean mane?"

"Why the fuck you ain't tell me KoKo supposed to be sick?" Face questioned pulling his pistol and holding it by his side.

"Whoa, mane!" B3 cried raising his hands in the air.

"On my kids mane, I ain't heard nothing like that mane. Don't let these niggaz get in your head mane because them same niggas be around here trying to fuck KoKo mane. That girl ain't sick mane." Face processed all that B3 uttered then tucked the pistol.

"Damn mane! You really just pulled yo' gun on me mane?" B3 implored in disbelief.

"If I found out otherwise… boy I gotta have you," Face threatened before hopping in the truck and pulling off.

***

Face had been nestling in the shower for thirty minutes with his thoughts.

"Could this bitch be that cruel? Would her mother allow her to pass this shit around knowingly? Shid…I might have

90

to kill this bitch... Maaan that nigga might be hatin' on a nigga..."

A knock on the door obstructed Face's thoughts.

"Yeah," he yelled outside of the shower curtain.

"Boy, get'cha ass out this shower! You been in here damn near an hour! You free now. You ain't got no reason to be in there whacking off!" Sierra quipped.

"Get the fuck away from the door," Face retorted, cutting the water off.

"Hurry the fuck up, nigga. I ain't got all day!" Sierra asserted banging on the door before walking away.

Face snuffled a laugh as he dried off. Fifteen minutes later, he stepped outside dipped in Givenchy and a few jewels.

"Bout damn time!" Sierra yelled pouring her shot of 1800.

"Fuck you want girl?" Face asked walking to the outside bar where Sierra and World were seated.

He locked Bs with World then took a shot from Sierra's bottle.

"I gotta take that rental back tomorrow," she stated.

Face reached into his pockets and handed her enough money to rent the truck for another month. Sierra took the money and shook her head.

"All this money you spendin', you could have got'chu a car," Sierra preached.

"I'on wanna hear that shit!" Face retorted batting the air with his hand dismissively.

"Aight, you gone be pawning ya lil jewelry in a minute," she added taking a shot.

World laughed.

"You gotta a real one fucked up!" Face assured.

Seconds later, his phone rang.

"Yeah?"

"Hey daddy! What'chu doing?" KoKo asked.

Face's mind reverted to Buger Bear's allegation. He collected himself before replying.

"Boolin' with my people. Wassup?"

"When you coming back over? I miss you," KoKo admitted chuckling seductively.

"Let me finish hollin' at my pepe, then I'm in ya chest."

"Okay, daddy. I gotta surprise for you too," KoKo pronounced happily.

"I'll be there."

Click! Face hung the phone up.

"Who that?" Sierra questioned being nosy.

Face hesitated before responding, "KoKo."

"KoKo?" Sierra face crinkled. "KoKo with the good hair-got a nice body?" Sierra implored.

"Yeah," Face admitted.

"Nigga, you tripping! All these hoes out here, nigga you fresh out!"

"Wassup sis? She sick or something?" Face removed a blunt from behind his ear and put flame to it.

"Nall, I ain't never heard nothin like that, but I heard she like to snort that good powder."

"Oh, yeah?" Face remarked blowing smoke from his nose.

"And they say she a lil thot thot," Sierra clowned taking another shot.

"Shit I'ma thot too," Face replied trying to make light of the situation.

"Bra, Bra like that project pussy! That savage life shit!" World added. "Let me hit the blunt," implied World reaching for it.

Face hit the blunt and passed it to World.

"I'm good, I'ma fuck wit y'all later," Face exclaimed locking Bs with World and kissing his sister on the cheek.

"Look at 'em, tender already," World claimed.

"I might be," Face admitted hopping in his rental and pulling off.

Chapter 14
Time To Go

When Face pulled up on 23rd, KoKo was outside sitting on her mother's porch. The moment she seen Face pulling up she made haste towards his truck excitedly. Face hopped out of the truck dipped in Givenchy. KoKo wrapped her arms around his neck and placed a tender kiss on his lips. She then stepped back to inspect his attire.

"Damn, daddy you sexy as fuck. Oh, my God, you got me so fuckin wet right now," KoKo admitted crossing her legs to contain the itch between her knees.

Face silently admitted that KoKo was also looking magically delicious.

"What's the surprise?" He asked dryly.

"Well damn, nice to see you too," she scoffed. "Come on," KoKo proclaimed grabbing Face by the hand and leading him to the apartment adjacent to her mother's.

Face noted all the nosy neighbors gawking at the fresh meat on the block before entering the apartment.

"Lexus!" KoKo called out.

Moments later, a light-skinned petite beauty appeared from the back of the apartment. Face quickly noted her hazel eyes, succulent lips, a tattoo of Tweety Bird on her right thigh, and the outrageous camel-toe sitting perfectly in her boy shorts.

"Bae, this is Lexus, my new roommate. Lexus this is who I was telling you 'bout, Face." KoKo introduced smiling uncontrollably.

"Wassup Lex?" Face greeted holding his hand out.

"Umm! Hey Face. You just make yourself right at home," Lexus exclaimed holding Face's hand longer than necessary while gazing in his eyes.

"Appreciate it," he retorted.

"Come on daddy," KoKo asserted pulling Face to the back of the apartment.

When Face entered the room rose petals littered the floor trailing to a king-size bed. Lit aroma therapy candles were scattered about the room, and a bottle of Remy on ice, and pre-rolled blunts were situated on the nightstand. Face secretly admired the set-up but showed no emotion. KoKo maintained a closed lipped smile as she led him to the left side of the bed and forced him in it. She removed his cocaine white Forces and low-cut socks, then alleviated his articles of clothing.

"I gotta holla at'chu bout something," Face stated above a whisper.

"Shhh…" KoKo chortled placing her index finger on his lips, then kissing them tenderly. "Relax daddy," she insisted opening the bottle of Remy and handing it to him.

After taking several shots, KoKo removed the bottle from his hands, placed it on the stand then lit a blunt. She took a few tokes then handed it to Face. He hit the blunt and came to the realization that Friday *When It Comes To You* was serenading beautifully in the room. Friday was of Face's favorite R&B artist. KoKo undressed, climbed in the bed and began to administer some of the slowest, intense head he'd ever had. She made love to his dick with her mouth while he smoked a blunt in a shimmery haze of bliss.

"Damn… this bitch right here maaan…" Face thought to himself gripping the sheets with one hand and the blunt in the other.

When his legs began to tremble, she applied more pressure until he released in her mouth.

"Ummm!" KoKo moaned as a load of warm semen flooded her mouth.

She continued to moan excessively until she was certain she'd drained him. KoKo's head was so severe that he couldn't even smoke the blunt properly. He had ashes everywhere. KoKo popped Face's dick from her mouth.

"You belong to me nah, I'ma make sho of that," she declared.

Before Face could respond, Lexus made her way into the room completely naked holding a heated bottle of flavored oil.

"How you feeling baby?" Lexus asked climbing in the bed eagerly.

"Appreciated," Face pronounced placing the blunt in the ashtray.

"As you should," Lexus assured.

She opened the bottle and gently poured the oil over Face's thighs, dick and balls. The warmth from the oil was sensational. KoKo and Lexus began to rub and massage the oil on and between his thighs, dick and balls. The feeling of having two different women with two different touches corresponding to accommodate his anatomy was pure Elysium. Lexus massaged and jacked Face's dick while KoKo massaged his balls and places kisses on his knee and thigh, Lexus licked her lips then wrapped them around Face's shaft and swallowed him whole.

"Ssss, Ooow…fffuck!" he moaned grabbing her ponytail.

Lexus wasted no time applying pressure, bobbing her head up and down rapidly.

"Umm, hmmm! Eat daddy dick up," KoKo taunted before placing his balls in her mouth.

"Ummmmmmmmm," Lexus moaned as she continued to bob her head and play with her clit.

"Feel good daddy?" KoKo implored.

"Ssss, ffffuck yeah! Sssshit!" He retorted through clenched teeth.

KoKo backed up, forced an arch in Lexus's back then proceeded to eat her pussy from behind.

"Hhhhhmmmmm!" Lexus moaned loudly and began to suck Face's dick demonically.

Moments later, Lexus was creaming in KoKo's mouth. After swallowing Lexus's nectar, KoKo grabbed Lexus by her hair and pulled her mouth away from Face's dick.

"Get up daddy," KoKo demanded then started kissing Lexus aggressively.

Face relocated behind Lexus while KoKo laid on her back and guided Lexus mouth to her love box. Lexus wasted no time latching on her clit while fingering her delicately.

"Ssss…ooow, yesss! Eat this pussy!" KoKo cried biting her bottom lip while looking up at Face.

Face grabbed his dick, spanked it on Lexus's ass cheek, then slid into her wet warm tightness.

"Sshit!" Face quipped, gripping her firm ass cheeks and sliding in and out of her sodden pussy.

Lexus stopped eating KoKo's pussy momentarily.

"Ooow, that dick good," Lexus declared looking back at Face before burying her face back into KoKo's fat pussy.

Face bit his lip and tilted his head back slightly giving him the perfect view of his dick going in and out of her pussy.

"Get that pussy daddy! Get, it, get it! Ooow, sshit, you better get it!" KoKo coached while grinding her pussy in Lexus face.

"Fffuck! This pussy wet!" Face admitted.

Lexus's pussy smacked loudly with each stroke. The trio's moans made music until all came to a climax.

"Sssshit! I'm skeeting in this pussy!" Face stated, fucking Lexus fast and hard.

"I'm nutting on that good dick…. Sssshit! Oooow, Yesss!" Lexus cried then latched back on to KoKo's clit.

"Ssss...Ooow...pussy skeeting!" KoKo cried cuming in Lexus's mouth.

After cuming inside of Lexus, Face pulled out, approached KoKo from the side, then slid wet dick in her mouth.

"Ummmm," KoKo moaned sucking Lexus juices from Face's dick while Lexus continued to eat her pussy.

Just the thought of Face fucking her face while getting her pussy ate turned KoKo on, forcing her to cum rapidly. Lexus swallowed everything KoKo's pussy dripped then made her way to Face's dick. She pulled his dick from KoKo's mouth and forced Face into a sitting position with his back against the headboard. Both women took turns placing Face's dick in and out of their mouths, driving him crazy. Face's legs shook while he gripped the sheets until he couldn't take the pressure no longer. He pulled Lexus's mouth from his dick then forced KoKo on her back. He grabbed both of her ankles, spread them horizontally, and proceeded to stroke her in a do or die manner.

"Whooo, daddy...you in this pussy!" KoKo screamed, pinching her nipples.

Lexus kissed and caressed KoKo while Face slipped in and out of KoKo's wetness perniciously.

"Ooooow...I'm nutting on that dick daddy!"

"Ffffffuck, I'm skeeting all in this pussy," Face announced as he and KoKo climaxed simultaneously.

Face collapsed on the bed chasing his breath while KoKo tried to contain shivering. Lexus left and re-appeared with a warm rag to clean KoKo and Face up. After wiping Face off, Lexus put his dick back into her mouth momentarily then cuddled up under him. Once KoKo gained her composure, she snapped.

"Umm, bitch! What the fuck is you doing?"

Lexus looked up at KoKo confused.

"Nothin, KoKo I'm just laying here," Lexus retorted.

"Play time over with! You can get the fuck out! Bye!" KoKo barked with a supercilious attitude.

"KoKo, what's the problem? I didn't do anything wrong," Lexus countered turning her palm upward in a feminine gesture.

"Hoe, that's my shit! The fuck I look like letting you cuddle up with my nigga. You done sucked and fucked, nah it's time to go!"

"Well, you don't have to be so rude and disrespectful about it," Lexus replied sadly as she left the room.

"Bitch dun lost her damn mind," muttered KoKo.

Face gazed at the ceiling wondering how many times have they done this; nevertheless, he enjoyed himself.

"You okay daddy?" KoKo implored rubbing and kissing Face's chest.

"Yeah I'm straight," he lied never looking her in the eyes.

"You lying. It's all over yo' face. Wassup daddy? Talk to me."

Face looked her in the eyes before speaking.

"Before I left you this morning, a nigga seen me and you hugged up. When you went back inside, he pulled up on me and told me not to fuck wit'chu kuz they say you sick."

KoKo put her head down and shook it from left to right.

"Say you use to fuck with a nigga from the bottom who got that shit," Face stated watching for a reaction.

"I used to fuck with a nigga from the bottom. Yeah that's true, but long after we broke up, he started fuckin wit this bitch name Mary; who's supposedly sick. Ain't shit wrong with me, this pussy A1," assured KoKo.

Face sat up to face her. "Look, just tell me the truth now and I ain't gone trip. I'm already fucked up bout'chu shid… We'll just die together," Face lied trying to see if her answer changed.

"Boy! Ain't shit wrong with me!" KoKo yelled then made haste to her dresser.

She removed a piece of paper and handed it to Face. He was relieved to see that it was KoKo's AIDS test with the results reading negative.

"Who pulled up on you and told you I was sick?" Questioned KoKo.

"It don't even matter. Your paper say negative," Face replied attempting to wrap his arms around her.

"Umm, Umm!" KoKo pronounced moving Face's arms. "Tell me."

"Buger Bear."

"Buger Bear?" KoKo repeated.

She chuckled with a closed lipped smile.

"Yeah. What'chu laughing for?"

"It's funny cuz that same nigga tried to holla at me this morning when you left," KoKo informed but forgot to mention that she sucked his dick for one hundred dollars.

"Oh, yeah?" Face implored with a demonic smirk.

"Yeah, bae. You can't tell these niggaz got in your head. They just want what'chu got daddy," KoKo convinced pushing Face backwards onto the bed.

She slipped his dick out and buried it deep in her throat taking him to a blissful state.

Chapter 15
Be Careful

Three weeks later, 10:35 p.m. at night…

KoKo was bending through the city in a Ford Taurus that Face had bought from an old white couple for $2800. She had her back windows up with the fronts down as she crept through the projects. When she turned on 31st, a male voice could be heard yelling her name. KoKo glanced in the rearview mirror and seen a man arms flailing about for her to turn around. She made her way around the corner and pulled alongside of the man who was so eager for her to turn around.

"Wassup, baby girl?" The man questioned leaning in the window with his 20 inch Cuban dangling.

Face grabbed his chin with his left hand and place his mini-Draco under his chin with his right hand.

"Buger Bear, my boy, wass poppin?"

Boc! Face drilled a bullet under Buger Bear's chin lifting his brain fragments through his scalp.

He snatched the Cuban before Bear dropped dead and KoKo pulled off precisely. Face had his seat laid all the way back, so Buger Bear never seen the Reaper coming.

"Pussy ass nigga," KoKo enunciated then turned the sounds of ESTGEE's *Water Zips* all the way up.

Sliding thru the streets/ took off my cleats and got some peace from it/ I been lit since I was selling water zips for 300/First time I hit something with that blik/ I had a weak stomach/7.62 bullets knock the numbers off a 300/ Heen died but his remaining life gone be a cucumber/Niggaz can't out snake me I'ma King Cobra/

When they made it back to the apartment, Face had barely made it through the door and KoKo was slipping his dick from his Amir's into her watering mouth. Face made a mental note that gangsta shit turned her on. He quickly locked the front door, then leaned his back against it while KoKo ate him up savagely.

"Ssss...fffuck! Since you wanna eat that dick up like that, I'm finna beat that pussy backwards!" Face groaned through clenched teeth.

He snatched KoKo by her hair and pulled her to a sofa.

"Get'cha ass up there," he demanded pushing her towards the sofa.

KoKo crawled on the sofa, got on her knees, opened her legs, and cocked her ass in the air. From this angle, he seen all of her. The sight of her dripping wet pussy caused his dick to flex. Face grabbed her wrist and pulled them behind her back causing her head to lean over the back of the couch. As he slid in, her knees trembled.

"Sss, ooow...Shit daddy," KoKo moaned, arching her back.

Seconds later, Lexus walked in completely naked and made herself comfortable on the couch next to KoKo. She leaned her back against the arm of the couch, spread her legs and began to finger fuck her clit.

"Damn this pussy biting," Face remarked picking up a steady pace

"Sss, ooow...yes!" KoKo cried throwing her pussy back.

Face fucked her rapidly, hard, and deep hitting her cervix from an intense angle, sending waves through her with every stroke.

"That's a good girl...fffuck! That's it, take this dick!"

"Daddy, you deep!" She yelled feeling dominated and submissive at the same time.

"Get that pussy," Lexus mumbled as she pinched her clit, moved her fingers up and down then into a massaging motion.

Clap! Clap! Clap! Clap! The sounds of KoKo's ass smacking against Face's thighs echoed throughout the apartment.

"Ooooow, daddy, sss…pussy skeeting!" KoKo cried as the pussy got wetter and constricted around Face's dick.

"Whoooooo, fffffuck, bitch I'm on my way!" Face moaned dumping his seeds deep inside of her phenomenal pussy.

"Ssss, ooooow…. Yes, I'm cuming," Lexus added, her legs shaking as she climaxed hard.

The trio found a place on the couch and basked in the aftershock of an orgasm.

***

Face awoke from a deep sleep by a warm sensation between his knees. When he gained consciousness fully, he seen that Lexus had his dick in her mouth.

"Lex? Fuck is you doing?" Face asked perturbed.

"I can't sleep, so you can't either," Lex stated then shoved his dick back in her mouth.

"You can't sleep?" Face implored his face creased. "Where KoKo at?"

Lexus shrugged her shoulders and kept sucking.

"Watch out, Lex! Move!" Face pronounced trying to remove her mouth from his dick.

"Um, Um!" Lex moaned with a vice-like grip.

Moments later, the front door could be heard shutting.

"Daddy!" KoKo called out making her way to the room.

Lexus quickly removed Face's dick from her mouth and headed to the nightstand. Face placed his dick back in his briefs and pretended to be sleep. KoKo entered the room and spotted Lexus.

"Bitch, what the fuck you doing in here?" KoKo snapped.

"I was just getting a lighter KoKo," Lexus lied holding up the lighter that she'd taken from the nightstand. "I'm not on nothing. You know I wouldn't try you like that," Lexus continued to lie walking past KoKo into the living room.

"Bitch dun lost her damn mind," KoKo mumbled then slid in bed with Face.

"Morning daddy. How you feeling?" She asked, rubbing his chest.

"Where you was at?" Face asked in a calm but intimidating tone.

"I was at mama's," KoKo interjected smoothly. "Well, I was trying to go to mama's but…"

"But, what?" Face snapped.

"It's this nigga I used to fuck with. He on mama porch talking to my brother, G-man. When I tried to walk in mama house, he was trying to talk and grab on me. I told him I got a nigga who don't fuck off, but he kept on, so I just came back over here."

Before KoKo could finish explaining, Face was already dressed heading out the door.

"Daddy!" KoKo sneered, jumping up to follow behind Face.

Face mobbed like the true stepper that he was over to Suga Moma's porch.

"Wassup, playboy?" Face questioned Ervin, peeping his attire.

Ervin was dipped in red with a Bulls hat on. Face figured he had to be a Blood but didn't give a fuck. About KoKo, it was up!

"Wassup bra?" Ervin retorted in a perplexed tone.

"You gotta get from round here homie," Face declared with a palliative smile.

When G-man seen KoKo following behind Face, he knew something sinister was at play.

"What?" Ervin implored with a screw face.

"Aye, chill my nigga, he over her with me," G-man pronounced attempting to pacify the situation.

"Nall, hold up G-man!" Ervin snapped placing the back of his hand on G-man's chest. "What'chu saying bra?" Ervin asked, stepping off the porch and pulling his pants up.

"Be careful," Face cantered.

Ervin sung a quick right that Face anticipated. All in one motion, Face stepped back drew his FN and squeezed off two shots.

Boc! Boc! Two hollowed tips with the dye pack slammed into Ervin's chest spinning and dropping him poetically.

"Da fuck?" G-man implored.

Boc! Boc! Stupid nigga!" Face exclaimed standing over Ervin before taking off behind the public housing apartments.

Neighbors who'd witnessed the murder quickly turned a blind eye and relocated inside their apartments. KoKo quickly trotted to her car, hopped in and pulled off. Face had slid through a hole in a gate that had been there for years and ended up on 24th Street. He spotted KoKo bending the corner. She pulled on the side of him, he hopped in, and they got in the wind. Face thought that he was standing on business unbeknownst to him that he'd just been manipulated to kill a man for nefarious reasons. KoKo wanted vengeance for Ervin's infidelities when they were together. While Face was asleep, KoKo had called Ervin and told him to come see her. He had no idea that fifteen minutes after leaving his house, he'd have four bullets in his ass.

Chapter 16
Say No Moe

After the murder, Face hid out at his sister's house in Lakewood Park. G-man had kept it solid and tole the fuzz that it was a robbery turned homicide. Fearing the repercussions the neighbors remained mute, but word silently fanned through the city that KoKo had a young tender Kold Killa wrapped around her finger. KoKo's fat warm pussy rested on the back of Face's neck as he laid between her legs smoking a blunt.

"You okay, daddy?" KoKo implored, massaging Face's scalp.

"Yeah, I'm straight," he retorted before his phone rang from and unknown number.

"Who the fuck is this?" Face barked.

He heard a familiar voice laugh before speaking.

"Wass popping killa?"

"Kream?" Face implored.

"The one and only!"

"Aaaah! Wass popping Bloody?'

"You already know, niggaz like us," Kream retorted.

"All the time. So, damn, what'chu out?"

"Nall, I bought a jack. They got me at Coleman Medium," Kream exclaimed.

"What they gave you?" Face questioned passing KoKo the blunt.

"Shid, I beat the attempt, but they gave me five for the dope."

"Glad you beat the attempt! Five years ain't shit though, you'll be back out here yesterday," Face enunciated.

"Yeah, I know. Listen though homie, ya hear me? I wanted to bark at'chu about something, ya hear me?"

"Talk to me."

"I been barking with the higher ups about giving me a sub-set, ya hear me?"

"Yeah!"

"It's looking real good, ya hear me? It's gone be A.M.G. Almighty Militant Gangstaz, ya hear me? Army fatigue bandanas, tied with red ones! Still, Bloody, ya hear me?"

"Hell yeah! I'm smelling that!"

"Listen, I wanted to know if you gone keep jacking Billy or roll over to this A.M.G. shit?" Kream offered.

"You already know, I'm wit'chu!" Face assured.

Kream laughed knowing that Face's loyalty was with him.

"That's wassup, Bloody. I'ma politic more with'chu later. I gotta hit my bitch up," Kream pronounced.

"Aight homie, two-twelve."

"Aye! I forgot to ask you. I heard you gotta older broad that got'chu pussy whipped!" Kream clowned.

Face laughed.

"I ain't gone kapp. I'm fucked up about her," he admitted.

Kream laughed.

"Ain't nothing wrong with it. Just stay focused, homie. Two-twelve!"

"All the time homie," Face retorted.

Click!

"Who was that daddy?" KoKo inquired, now massaging Face's shoulders.

"Oh, that was my big fool."

"What'chu mean?"

"My big homie," Face exclaimed, lighting another blunt.

"You mean, like...yo blood homie?"

"Yeah," Face pronounced, blowing smoke from his nose.

"Oh, okay."

Face laughed loudly.

"What'chu laughing for?" KoKo asked smiling.

"I was just thinking about how you was riding my dick screaming Suwoop," he enunciated, passing KoKo the blunt.

KoKo laughed shamelessly. "When I was ridin' that dick, I was like, damn this Blood dick good...so yeah I said it," Koko explained with a sexy laugh.

"How you knew I was Blood?" Face implored, passing the blunt to KoKo.

"I did my due diligence," KoKo replied, placing a kiss on Face's shoulder.

"Oh, yeah?"

"Umm huh."

Moments later, Sierra walked into the room.

"Brah, Moses wanna holla at'chu," Sierra informed.

"Aight, I'm comin' nah," said Face, getting up from between KoKo's thighs.

"Heyy, Sierra," KoKo spoke with more emphasis than necessary.

"Wassup, KoKo," Sierra retorted with a tepid smile.

She wasn't too fond of her brother dealing with KoKo but kept the peace out of love for her brother.

"You aight in here? You need anything?"

"You ain't got no liquor?"

"Yeah, come on," Sierra retorted.

Face headed to the back patio where he found Moses counting money. Moses was Sierra's man and weed kingpin of the city. He had seen Face around a few times and knew him by reputation, and Face knew Moses by his reputation of getting money.

"Face, boy wass hadnin?" Moses greeted holding a bejeweled hand out.

Face locked fingers with him and had a seat across from him.

"Wass poppin?" Face retorted.

"Chasing paper, my nigga. That's what this shit about…paper," Moses stated, sitting a stack of bills on the table before continuing his count of another.

Remy and Patron bottles littered the table along with exotic weed blunts.

"Help yourself to any of this shit on the table bra," Moses offered.

Face took a shot of Remy, then rolled himself a joint.

"So, what'chu wanted to bark at me about?" Face questioned, lighting his blunt.

"Yo' sister love you, bra. When you was up the road, she talked about'chu all the time. Now, that'chu home, I wanted to see if you wanna get this paper," Moses offered.

Face was just pondering all week where his next dollar would come from and now opportunity had just landed in his lap.

"Hell yeah, I'm wit it!" Face assured assertively.

"Say no moe. We out'chere!" Moses quipped.

***

Three days later…

Moses had given Face ten pounds of loud and a burner phone with bookoo clientele on it. He even gave Face the money for a spot to trap out of. Face settled on a spot that was next to the Brown store and across the street from another store called The One Stop Shop. It was a small complex building that small time hustlers dubbed The Carter. The building had five apartments at the bottom, five on the top, and was one way in and one way out. Face rented the middle apartment at the top, so that he could see everything coming and going. His first day of opening up a shop, he'd moves two of the pounds easily on the breakdown tip. Instead of KoKo being supportive, she showed pangs of jealousy.

"Um, don't 'chu think you movin' a lil fast?" You just got out of prison, and you got all this traffic coming to the spot," KoKo complained, her face semi-twitching as she made periodic sniffles.

Face joviality vanished as he screwed his face and gazed at her thoughtfully before replying.

"Bitch, I just bodied two niggaz bout'chu and you got the audacity to complain about me getting this paper? Hoe you tripping! And why the fuck yo' mouth twitching and shit? You snorting that shit?" Face snapped.

KoKo lapsed into a simmering silence before winding her way around the table to where Face was seated counting.

"You right, I'm sorry daddy," KoKo enunciated in the most seductive voice she could muster. "I'm just scared you might leave me when you come up," she admitted, pulling a gram and a key from her bra.

She took a one in each nostril, straddled Face's lap and placed the key full of coke to his nose.

"I love you daddy, Please forgive me."

Face snorted the coke then gazed at her ambivalently.

KoKo unsaddled Face's lap, then pulled his dick out. To Face's astonishment, she sprinkled a hefty line of coke across his dick then snorted it off. She then gazed into his eyes as she swallowed him whole and continued to suck him in an artful manner for a convivial hour. When KoKo was done, she'd sucked all Face's ability to decipher logic from his dick.

Chapter 17
Stupid Bitch

Four days later, Face had paid Moses $10,000 and grabbed 10 more pounds. Moving ounces for two hundred a piece, he had made $32,000. Face gave Moses ten racks and used the twelve racks to buy him a whip and fix his apartment up. He was outside sitting on the trunk of his red Mercury when a white Jimmy GMC pulled up and let the driver's window down. Face snatched his pistol from his Balmain's but tucked it once he seen that it was a beautiful ebony queen,

"So, you just gone shoot me huh?" Implored the beautiful woman.

"It depends," Face retorted, approaching the truck.

"Depends on what, sexy?" She flirted.

"It depends on your reason for pullin' up, beautiful," Face cantered, smiling mischievously.

"You got some loud?"

"What'chu need?"

"Let me get a eighth," she said, reaching for her money.

Face leaned in his car and grabbed a half.

"Here, you straight. Next one on you," Face exclaimed passing her the half.

"Thank you. You might as well get my number. I'm Quanda."

Face got the number and logged her in.

"Aight Quanda, I'm Face."

"Who the fuck is this hoe?" KoKo yelled walking up.

"Bye, Face," Quanda pronounced, pulling off slowly. "Thanks for the weed," she stated out of the window before disappearing into traffic.

"Who the fuck was that?"

"She bought some weed," Face answered.

"How you know her?" KoKo impulsively shouted.

"I don't. She just pulled up."

"For now on, I serve the hoes, and you serve the niggas! Got me fucked up! I ain't stupid!" She snapped.

"Man take yo' fuck ass in the house! You out here causing a scene trying to fuck a nigga money up!"

"You heard what I said!" KoKo proclaimed, walking off.

"Fuck out my face, stupid ass bitch!"

"I got'cha bitch," she assured, turning around rushing Face with a barrage of punches.

Face side stepped them and slapped spittle from her mouth.

KoKo held her face in disbelief. "Ooow bitch! You gon' get fucked up for this!" KoKo threatened.

"Whatever, hoe!

KoKo made haste towards their apartment.

"Stupid bitch!" Face mumbled.

Moments later, an outrageous red Tahoe pulled up and two young niggaz hopped out with guns drawn. Face attempted to reach for his pistol but was slow on the draw.

"Today, a good day to die, ana? Reach again nigga!" A youngin by the name of Shooter dared.

"Get in the truck," the other youngin by the name of Lil Fif God demanded.

"Y'all lil niggaz gotta a real nigga fucked up! If you gone squeeze nigga squeeze nah kuz I ain't getting in that truck!"

Seconds later, the back window rolled down and Face laid eyes upon one of the most gorgeous women he'd ever seen.

"Step into my office, this won't take long," she assured.

Face glanced at the two youngins then made his way into the truck. He noted that the woman had long red dreadz, hazel eyes and deep dimples.

"Damn this bitch beautiful," Face thought to himself.

"What'chu name is man?" She inquired.

"Face,"

"Face, I'm Assata."

He looked at her thoughtfully as her name registered in his mental. Face had heard her name being thrown around the prison when he was up the road.

"Wass popping?" Face implored.

Wass popping is…it's been brought to my attention that'chu operating in Blood territory, homie. Nah, normally I would have handled a bituation like this with less words, but I'm in a good mood today. I'ma give you a chance to close shop or pay taxes. You decide," Assata proclaimed.

Face looked her in her eyes. "I'm Billy. 9 Trey Gangsta," Face informed.

"You, Billy, huh?" Assata implored.

"Black Wall Street," Face retorted proudly.

"Revolutionary reflection," Assata replied smiling. "Who you walk with?"

"Kream."

"Kream? Kream, that's the homie. He gotta lil Fed beef right?"

"Yeah, he ain't got long."

Assata shook her head in agreement.

"Listen, my apologies homie, and I'on do that often. You the homie, so you good. Keep running' ya lil operation and just patch in once a month till Kream touchdown. Take my math," Assata insisted, giving Face her number.

"You need anything from me, hit me."

"Aight."

Two-twelve damu," Assata enunciated.

"All the time," Face retorted, stepping out of the vehicle.

Face watched the Tahoe pull off and thought about how them lil niggaz had the drop on him. He chuckled them sat on the trunk of his whip.

***

Hours later, Face entered the apartment and was quickly enveloped with a delightful stench. He made his way to the kitchen and found KoKo over the stove. They locked eyes.

"Dinner ready, daddy. You hungry?" Questioned KoKo as if nothing occurred.

Face gazed at her contemplatively.

"This bitch prolly dun put period blood or some type of poison in the food." Face pondered.

"Nall, not right nah," he retorted, pulling his money out to count it.

"Well I already put'cha a plate in the oven, I'm finna head to Mama house to grab the rest of my stuff. You need anything while I'm out?"

"Yeah grab me a bottle of 1738 and some cigars," Face exclaimed, handing her a hand full of bills.

"Okay, be right back, daddy." KoKo grabbed her keys off the table, kissed Face then left.

"Crazy bitch," mumbled Face.

His phone rang seconds later,

"Yeah?"

"Damn Bloody! Since you been wit'cha lil cougar bitch, yeen been fuckin wit lil bra," World declared.

Face chuckled,

"A bitch flick ya lil balls the tight way and you all in love nah! You fresh out bra, you supposed to be doggin' shit out, not cuffing!"

"Watch ya mouth," warned Face.

"Look at'cha! In ya body kuz I called her a bitch. You in violation homie," World clowned.

113

"I can't be violated nigga! Um hmm! But n'all doe, I just been trying to run it up. I'ma get up wit'cha," Face promised.

"I already know wass popping. Moses dropped it on me too. I got Ave S swanging!" World proclaimed. "Yeah, I forgot too nigga. I seen ya lil boo thang in the Elks looking like a whole snack."

"Who?"

"Terrelle! She was with a nigga too," World disclosed.

"Damn! I ain't talk to her in a minute," Face stated before his phone beeped. "Aye bra hold on, I got another call."

"Hell nawl, just fuck with me later," World said.

"Aight, two-twelve bra."

"All the time," World cantered.

Face clicked over.

"Yeah?"

"Bra, wassup wit'chu man?"

"Who the fuck is this?" Face snapped.

"G-man!"

"Fuck you mean?" Face implored.

"Mothafuckaz calling me telling me you and my sister all out in the open fighting and shit."

"And you hit my line to say what?"

"Bra, I know how my sister is. All I'm saying is y'all take that shit in the house. Don't be in public wit that shit," advised G-man.

"Wherever she start it at, I'm a finish it," Face cantered with his voice sharp.

G-man exhaled deeply. "Bra!"

"Maaaaan…!"

Click! Face hung the phone up. "Fuck off my line with that shit," Face barked.

***

When Face awoke, he glanced at his watch and realized that he'd dozed off for two and a half hours. His watch read 11:30 p.m.

"KoKo!" He yelled, rising from his seat at the kitchen table to inspect the rest of the apartment.

He looked in both rooms and found them empty.

"Fuck this bitch at?" He mumbled, pulling his phone out to call her. He called three times only to get her voicemail.

"Aight bitch," he stated, grabbing his pistol and car keys to leave.

Face hopped in his whip and drove by KoKo's mother and Lexus apartment, but her car was nowhere in sight. After calling and getting the voicemail again, Face just drove through the city, sipping out of a bottle of Remy with his pistol on his lap listening to Mya's *Ridin'*. Mya's song was playing, but Face was remixing it as it played.

I'm riding, I'm riding/Pass yo' mama's house/You got me riding, I'm riding/Pass Lexus house/You got me riding, I'm riding/Hoe I'm finna kill you/ Bitch you got me riding dirty/Looking for you I.../

Face's phone rung, fucking up his remix. He turned the music down and answered it.

"Yeah?"

"Wassup big bra, where you at?" Sierra asked concerned.

"I'm just bending through the city. Wass popping?" Face implored.

"You by yo'self?"

"Yeah, wassup?"

"Ride down S, I wanna show you something," Sierra exclaimed.

"Shid, I'm on 25th right nah."

"Let me know when you on Avenue S," Sierra advised.

Face made a left turn on Avenue T them made his way around the curve,

"I'm on S right na, sis. I'on see you."

"On S where?"

115

"In front of Mama house."

"Keep goin'," she advised.

"Fuck you got going on?" Implored Face, making his way down Avenue S.

When Face drove past a few more houses, something caught his attention.

"Da fuck?" Face quipped.

"You see it?" Sierra questioned.

"Yeah, I got it," Face retorted with his voice dripping asperity.

"I just left Mama house, I'm home. I just wanted you to see that shit for yaself," Sierra remarked.

"Good looking, sis. I love you."

"Love you too, bra. Call me tomorrow."

"Bet," Face retorted hanging up the phone.

Clear as day KoKo's car was parked outside of Robert's house. He crept by slowly as a million ways to kill them both pervaded his mind. His first thought was to lurk in the shadows and catch them both coming out of the house, but he quickly dismissed that thought for one more sinister. Face kept it pushing and headed home.

Chapter 18
A Kold Killa

It was thirty minutes after two a.m. when KoKo slipped into the apartment.

"Bae," she called out just above a whisper closing the door behind her.

Tiptoeing into the darkness, she hit her shin on the coffee table causing noise to echo throughout the apartment.

"Fuck," she whimpered, rubbing her shin rapidly to contain the pain.

"Daddy," KoKo called out as she rounded the wall that led to their bedroom.

Crack!

Face hit KoKo square in the jaw, dropping her rigorously. Before her mind could register what just took place, Face was dragging her into the bathroom where a tub of bleach water awaited her. He leaned her against the tub and slapped her back to reality.

"Bae, what'ch do…" KoKo's words were cut short as Face submerged her underwater.

"Bitch, I'll kill ya," Face threatened through clenched teeth, leaving her under for fifteen seconds before bringing her back up.

He allowed her to gasp and draw in one deep breath before taking her back under. She clawed at his arms as the bleach burned her eyes intensively.

"Fuck ass hoe," he barked leaving her under for another ten seconds before bringing her back up. "I'm ask you one time! Where the fuck you was?" Face questioned, his eyes depicting something demonic.

KoKo gasped, chasing her breath, She could taste the bleach in her lungs and felt as if she was on the brink of passing out. Her tears blended with the water as she gathered herself to answer Face's question.

"I was at Lexus…"

Face submerged her back under, spilling water all over the floor. Twenty seconds later, he snatched her up.

"Clean all this water off my fuckin' floor," Face demanded and turned to leave while KoKo gasped for air and became vomitous.

After catching her breath, she spoke. "I didn't even do nothing!" KoKo lied through fake tears.

Face ignored her cries as he lay stolidly in bed, gazing at the roof.

Thirty minutes later KoKo had cleaned the vomit and water up and took a hot shower. She emerged from the bathroom and found Face gazing at the ceiling pensively with both hands behind his head. KoKo brazenly crawled into the bed and laid her head on Face's chest. She wasn't sure if Face really knew where she was but in her sick twisted mind…. Face's attempt to kill her was a display of love.

***

Face sat impassively in the bathroom snorting coke. He'd been in there for three hours before he heard the front door open and close. A male's voice could be heard conversing with a woman as the sound of footsteps became closer.

"Maan, you tripping! I'm telling you that nigga don't know shit!" The familiar voice stated, walking in the bedroom next to the bathroom.

Face slipped out of the bathroom stealthily with a Machete in hand.

"Heen livin' like that! Maaan, I'm call you back! *Click!*

"Stupid azz bitch!"

"Wass popping?" Face implored.

Robert spun around grabbing his pistol out of pure instinct to no avail. Face swung the Machete with acute precision severing half of his arm from his body. Robert's severed hand was still clutching his pistol as it laid bloody in front of him to see.

Ahhhhh!" Robert screamed in shock.

Face swung again placing a deep crevice into his shoulder. Robert fell to the ground, pleading as Face stood over him.

"Come on, my nigga! Not about no hoe!" Robert cried as spurts of blood shot from his limb.

Face pointed the Machete in his face. "I hear you…but my reality is different from yours. This shit deeper than what'chu perceiving," Face philosophized before brutally chopping Robert into human strips.

Robert's blood was splattered all over Face as he ransacked the spot. He made out with a pound of weed, a little cash, and some jewelry.

***

Three days later…

News had fanned throughout the city that Robert's mother had found him decapitated in his room. She expressed to the authorities and the media that she believed her son had dealings with a cartel and had run off with their product..

"It's a lot of senseless killing taking place in the city of Fort Pierce, Florida but never to this degree. If one looks at the very nature of this horrific crime, it's apparent that some mob or cartel had a hit out on my son. Robert, my only son was left butchered and nearly unidentifiable. That's not the work of some street gang punk! But I'ma tell you like this, you're not running me away from my house! You hear me?" Robert's mother stated, looking and pointing into the camera.

KoKo studied Face intently from the passenger's seat of his car while he sat impassively smoking a blunt in the driver's seat, watching Robert's mother interview. She found it no coincidence that Robert was killed the night after she had seen him and unbeknownst to Face, Robert was the same nigga that KoKo had violated her house arrest to go see. She had told Robert that Face was her new nigga, but he couldn't care less. He had begged KoKo for one last slice of her prestigious pie, which she agreed. The end result was death by mutilation. Face looked to his right and caught KoKo gazing at him.

"You aight?" Face inquired with a demonic lopsided grin, visibly forced and uneasy but as expected acquiescent.

"Yeah, I'm good daddy," she retorted with a pallid smile.

"You sho?" Face asked again, putting his car in gear and pulling out of his mother's driveway.

"Um huh," she murmured.

"Okay," Face pronounced, stopping in front of Robert's mother's house.

He glanced at Koko before hopping out and knocking on the front door. Moments later the door opened, and Robert's mother stepped out.

"Hey, Ms. Rita. My condolences," Face expressed hugging her tightly around the waist as she did the same to his neck.

"Thank you, baby. They killed my Robby, Face," Ms. Rita cried.

Ms. Rita loved Face like her own. He was Robert's childhood friend and would come by to check on her occasionally.

"If you need anything just call me," Face declared pulling the same $3500 he'd taken from Robert from his pocket and handed it to her.

"Thank you, Face," Ms. Rita retorted, kissing Face on the cheek.

KoKo watched Face console Robert's mother as he reacted with counterfeit anger, disgust, and all the justifiable emotions of losing a loved one. She became strangely emaciated and terrified simultaneously as she came to the conclusion that Face had an insatiable appetite for murder. Her heartrate increased as did the intense itch between her legs as Face made his way back to the vehicle. KoKo crossed her legs and bit her bottom lip.

Chapter 19
A Good Night To Die

A month later, all was cordial with KoKo and Face. They had intense copulation, ate, and more copulation with no kind of discrepancies. Everything was so vibrant that Face decided to pop out with KoKo to a club dubbed The Elks. It was an infamous hole-in- the-wall and considered a death trap due to its location. The Elks sat in the heart of the city between two rival gangs, which explains the carnage.

It was a soft summer Friday night, the crowd thick and boisterous with sensuous beauty everywhere. KoKo stepped out with her natural hair layered, a tight fitted Givenchy dress that showed her whole right hip, some stud ringed stilettos by Givenchy, and her nails and toes were freshly manicured with gel tips. Face decided to keep it Gangsta and simple. He wore a pair of red Bally Champion sneakers, fatigue joggers, a V-neck, and fatigue Bulls cap. He also was draped in a few jewelz that had the thotys gawking. The toxic duo grabbed two blue Long Island Ice Teas and found a table near the floor.

"You lookin' sexy as fuck, daddy," KoKo whispered in Face's ear then placed a wet kiss on his lips.

"You too," Face retorted, kissing her again before putting flame to his blunt.

KoKo placed her clutch on the table, grabbed her drink, and stood in front of Face twerking to Sexy Red's *Get It Sexy.*
Get it Sexy/Get it Sexy/

Get it Sexy/Get it Sexy

KoKo twerked like she was riding a dick while onlookers watched and passed judgement. Face noted it but could care less. He did a quick circumspection around the crowded club and didn't see any real threats. He laughed when he spotted Herman in a cut hugging the wall. He hadn't seen Herman since the day World shot him in the ass.

"Mane, wassup, mane?"

Face looked to his left and spotted B3 standing next to him.

"Wass popping?" Face retorted.

"Look mane! The whole club watching you and KoKo, mane!" B3 informed.

"As they should," Face cantered, blowing smoke from his nose.

"Talk yo' shit then, mane!" B3 spoke.

KoKo waved at B3 then kept twerking. Face handed B3 the blunt then stood up.

"Bae, I'm finna go to the restroom," Face said in KoKo's ear.

She shook her head, okay.

"Aye B3, watch KoKo till I come back."

"I got'chu, mane," B3 assured, posting up next to KoKo.

Face slithered through the crowd and into the men's room. It was so small that only two could occupy it at a time. Face took a bump of coke in each nostril then slid it back in his Newport box behind the plastic. He wiped his nose and was preparing to leave out when the door opened, and a beautiful young woman strolled in and locked the door.

"Umm! Wassup, Face?"

"Wass poppin, CC?" Face retorted with a quizzical expression.

CC boldly closed the space between them and grabbed a handful of Face's dick.

"This dick," CC replied, biting her bottom lip.

"I thought'chu don't fuck in bathrooms, remember?" Face exclaimed with a luminous smile.

"Man, fuck all that. You keep dodging and shit, so I'm finna get this dick nah!" CC pronounced, pulling Face's semi-hard dick from his joggers.

"Your sister out there, girl!" Face warned.

"She good. B3 keeping her company," she proclaimed then slid Face's dick into her mouth while gazing into his eyes.

"Shhhit!" He cried.

"Umm huh," CC taunted, bobbing her head relentlessly.

Her head was just as fierce as KoKo's and was on the verge of bringing Face to a premature climax. CC felt Face grow longer in her mouth. She snatched him out of her mouth, stood up and bent over the sink, hiking her mini skirt up.

"Damn," Face muttered, noting that CC didn't have on any panties.

He grabbed his dick and guided it into her wet tight-fitting canal.

"Oooow!" They both moaned in tandem.

Once Face was deep inside, he grabbed both of her butter soft ass cheeks and began rapidly stroking.

"Ssss, oow, fffuck…this dick good!" CC cried, gripping the sink.

"Umm huh," Face added biting his bottom lip as the site of her pretty succulent ass cheeks was bouncing off his thighs excited him.

"Ssshit! Um nutting in this pussy," Face announced, beating CC's pussy backwards.

"Sss, ooow, yesss! Nut all in this good pussy," CC retorted cuming while throwing her pussy back as she felt Face releasing in her.

"Grrrrr…Aaaaaahh…Ssshit!" Face growled as the climax made his knees buckle.

"Damn, girl!" He cried, pulling his dick out of her wet pussy.

"I know," CC replied then turned around to suck the nectar from his swipe.

"You know you chose wrong. It is what it is thought," CC voiced as she stood to wet some tissue to clean her pussy.

"You right, but I'm standing on my choice. Appreciate the box, but I gotta slide. Get up with me," Face enunciated and slid out of the men's room.

On his way back to his table, he seen B3 trying his best to keep the hyenas off of KoKo as she continued to twerk with perfection.

"It's a good night to die, ana?" Face yelled approaching the scene.

When they seen that it was Face, they tucked their tails and retreated to another location.

"Boy them niggas was on her mane!" B3 stated way past tipsy.

"Good looking out," Face quipped.

"Heyy daddy," KoKo said stopping her twerking to wrap her arms around his neck and kiss him.

Face reciprocated kissing her back, grabbing hands full of her soft nerf ass cheeks.

"Wassup sis?" CC greeted with a slight pang of jealousy.

Face glanced at CC pensively. He contemplated her intentions. Face had no idea that KoKo and CC had an ongoing tit-for-tat feud of fucking each other's man. They loved each other dearly but couldn't seem to break that tit-for-tat ritual.

"Heyy, CC," KoKo retorted hugging CC's neck while CC gazed at Face lustfully.

"Hey Face," CC spoke.

"Wass popping, sis?" he retorted. "You need a drink," he offered.

"I'm good, thank you though."

Just as Face thought things couldn't get more uncomfortable, Meka and KiKi approached with extremely bad colored wigs and attire,

"Pussy nigga! This what'chu do? Fall in the club with bottom of the barrel ass hoez? And then yo' trifling azz put that dick on my daughter? Your ass need to be shot in the head!" Meka enunciated with KiKi standing beside her perturbed.

"Bottom of the barrel?" KoKo inquired.

"Garbage, KoKo. Hoe you garbage!" Meka assured.

"If I'm garbage, hoe trash me then!" KoKo dared.

"Hoe you slangin' pussy from here to Gifford and everywhere else!" Meka continued

Whap!

KoKo hit Meka square in the mouth, dropping her instantly.

Whap!

CC hit KiKi in the jaw and followed up with a rapid combination. KiKi stumbled but was a little on the heavy side, making it hard for CC's featherweight punches to drop her. KiKi grabbed a handful of CC's hair and began trading punches with her. KoKo stopped the onslaught on Meka and helped CC defeat KiKi, pulling her to the ground. An unknown man attempted to break up the fight and Face blindsided him with a swift right, dropping him. B3 chimed in and stomped his head in the floor. Finally, security came, grabbed KoKo and CC and carried them out the door with Face and B3 behind them. Once outside, security was a little too ruff with KoKo. Face pulled his CM-40 micro compact .40 caliber pocket rocket that security missed on the search and pointed it at his face.

"This job worth your life, stupid nigga?" Face questioned with blood in his eyes and death in his heart.

"N'all, man I'm sorry! Security pleaded with his arms in the air.

"Shoot that bitch ass nigga in the face, daddy!" KoKo provoked.

Right when Face was about to squeeze, he noted the cops that secured the club area on the let out approaching the street. He quickly tucked his pistol and grabbed KoKo.

"Yall be safe out here," Face warned as he left the scene with B3 and CC close behind.

Chapter 20
I Missed You Too

After the club Face and KoKo fucked like porn stars until sunrise. It was now 8:25 a.m. and they were still at it.

"Sss..ooow, ffuck! Yess, give me this dick!" KoKo moaned through clenched teeth with both hands around Face's throat as she rode and bounced on his dick chaotically.

Face had his hands around her wrist thrusting upwards meeting her halfway.

"Sss…ooow...pussy, skeetin! Sss…pussy skeetin, daddy…fffuck!" KoKo cried as she creamed all over Face's dick.

Face came right behind her. She removed her hands from around Face's neck and placed them on his chest as she grinded all the nut from her and Face's body. Face was in pure bliss as he chased his breath. KoKo climbed off of Face and cleaned his dick with her mouth. When she was done she cuddled up next to him. They both lapsed into a simmering silence until KoKo busted it up.

"Daddy," KoKo quipped, rubbing on Face's chest.

"Wassup?" Face retorted.

"What that hoe was talking bout when she said you put that dick on her daughter?"

Face gazed at her for a moment before speaking.

"I used to fuck Meka before I met'chu. One day, she asked me to go bond her daughter outta jail. When I went to pick her daughter up. she was all over me, and I end up fuckin her. Me and Meka wasn't no couple or nothing, so I ain't owe her no loyalty. Plus, she was selling pussy in Gifford, so it is what it is," Face voiced.

KoKo shook her head in disgust. "You was fucking the mama and the daughter. That dick don't discriminate," KoKo clowned.

Face looked at KoKo like she was crazy. "What she meant by you slangin' pussy from here to Gifford?"

"Oh, Lord! Here you go," KoKo tried to deflect.

"N'all, nigga! Answer the question!" Face snapped.

KoKo exhaled with exaggeration. "I use to fuck with a nigga that she was fuckin with. She just bitter kuz the nigga left her for me, and I didn't even want the nigga," KoKo enunciated.

"Yeah, aight," Face cantered.

"Look, I don't wanna argue, daddy. I love you, nigga," KoKo admitted, placing a kiss on Face's lips.

"Love you too," Face retorted.

"Nah, let's go to Wal-Mart, I wanna make us a big breakfast," she declared, getting up to hop in the shower.

"Bae, get up and come get in the shower with me!" KoKo yelled.

Face crawled out of bed and heard a knock at the door.

"I'm coming," he told KoKo putting on some briefs to go answer the door.

On his way to the door, he could hear KoKo singing in the shower. He opened the front door, cracking it a little.

"Hey handsome," Quanda greeted smiling.

Face looked back to make sure KoKo was still in the shower. "What'chu doing? Why you ain't call me," Face whispered.

"I did call. Your phone going to voicemail."

"What'chu need?"

"I want a half ounce," Quanda replied, reaching in the door grabbing a handful of Face's dick.

"Umm!" She moaned.

"Bae!" KoKo called out.

"Give me the money," Face whispered.

Quana slipped Face seventy-five dollars. Face made haste to the kitchen and grabbed a half from the kitchen cabinet.

"I'm coming, nah!" He yelled to KoKo while slipping Quanda the weed.

"Call me," Quanda whispered.

Face threw thumbs up and closed the door, locking it before heading to the shower.

"What was you doing?" KoKo inquired, her face tightened with emotion.

"You ain't hear the door? Somebody wanted some weed," Face cantered, smoothly grabbing her washcloth from her hands.

He kissed her then proceeded to wash her thoroughly.

"I love you, nigga," KoKo proclaimed, gazing at Face in a sneaky seductive manner.

"A nigga love your ass too," Face admitted, cleaning her pussy before kneeling and sucking a mouthful.

***

Wal-Mart was busy and crowded with mostly beautiful women with children when Face and KoKo entered.

"Bae I gotta taste for steak and salad. Maybe some shrimps," KoKo announced, pulling her tight boy shorts out of her fat coochie before grabbing a buggy. "What'chu think daddy," she added making sure her ass jiggled as she pushed the buggy.

"You know I'm fucked up about salad and steak, I got taste for some cheesecake too," he asserted, grabbing a handful of her pillow soft booty.

"Umm, you love this ass don't'chu?" KoKo inquired seductively.

"Nigga you love this dick!" Face retorted.

"Sholl do," she admitted, reaching out to grab a handful of Face's dick.

A white couple walking by seen the indecent public display of affection and scurried off with a snuffle of disdain.

"Aight nah, make a nigga bend ya ass over in one of deez freezers," Face declared.

"Come get it then, tough ass nigga," KoKo dared, opening a freezer full of frozen pizza and sticking her head inside while twerking.

Face slapped her right ass cheek aggressively.

"Oow!" She moaned biting her bottom lip.

"Stop playing and brang your crazy ass on. I'm missing all kind of money. Let's grab this shit and go!"

"Nigga you started it!" KoKo retorted, grabbing the buggy and pushing it.

"I got'chu when we get home," Face promised as they turned down the meat aisle.

As soon as they made it into the aisle, Face locked eyes with a familiar face and they both lit up with the biggest smile their faces could shape. KoKo glanced back and forth at the unknown woman and Face.

"Bitch! What the fuck you smiling for?" KoKo snapped.

"Hoe, I can smile if I want to, bitch! You got me fucked up!" Kierra declared.

KoKo attempted to rush Kierra, but Face stepped between them.

"Who the fuck is this hoe, Face? And why you trying to save her?"

"You wanna go to jail for fighting in Wal-Mart?" He asked.

"Fuck all that! Who is she, Face?"

"That's just my lil homie. Knew her way before we met," he stated evenly.

"Fuck that!" KoKo spat, trying with everything in her to get to Kierra, while Kierra bore a dazzling smile, but Face refused to let KoKo engage.

"You know what? Fuck you, pussy ass nigga!" KoKo spat and rushed off leaving the buggy.

"I didn't mean to get'chu in trouble, but that bitch is outta pocket," Kierra proclaimed.

"You straight. How you doin' though?" Face inquired hugging Kierra and kissing her on the cheek.

"One day at a time, you know. Surviving."

"I'm feelin that," Face retorted, gazing deep into her soul.

"Listen, go check ya girl. We'll catch up later," Kierra advised.

"You right. I'ma hit'chu asap," Face assured then trotted off.

When he made it outside, he didn't see KoKo car nowhere in sight.

"Fuck it!"

Face headed back inside and found Kierra.

"She left you?" Kierra asked.

"Yeah, I ain't trippin' though. I was kinda hoping she did," Face admitted.

"And why is that?"

"Kuz a nigga miss you anyway," Face stated in all seriousness.

Kierra smiled and exhaled. "I missed you too."

Chapter 21
You Gone Learn

It was a little after 3:30 a.m. Face and Kierra were laid up at the Quality Inn wrapped in each other's arms. To Kierra's astonishment, Face had took his time with every inch of her celestial body and made unforgettable passionate love to her. He wanted his appreciation for her code of silence to be solidified in her mind, body, and soul. Guilt weighed heavy on Face's heart and his twisted mind, making love to her brought him solace.

"Wassup wit'chu Face? Everything aight?" Kierra inquired concerned.

"Yeah, I'm good. Why you ask?" Face retorted, kissing her on her cheek as she lay snuggled next to him.

"Kuz, I know you like to go ham in a bitch pussy. Nigga you just made love to me, like you love me. Nah, we both know Cupid ain't got'chu in his cross hairs, so wassup?" Kierra pointed out.

Face inhaled deeply before exhaling. A few seconds passed before he replied.

"I do got love for you. I'm not in love wit'chu, but I do have an abundance of love for you. You coulda put me and my brother in a position to where we coulda never seen daylight again, but'chu kept it solid. For that, I gotta slew of love for you. As for me making love to you, that was me obliging."

"Whateva nigga," Kierra remarked, playfully hitting Face on the arm.

"N'all though, real talk. I feel guilty for not protecting you," Face expressed.

"Get off that guilt trip shit. I'm way past that, and I'll be glad when you get past it too. Face, I ain't no punk ass bitch. I'm really that!" She assured.

"Respect," Face cantered, nodding his head.

"While we at it, wassup wit'chu and KoKo?"

"What'chu mean?"

"Da fuck is you doing fucking with a hoe like that? Face, I'm 18 and niggas my age be talkin' about how they done fucked and ran a train on that hoe. That bitch a whole prostitute. Face you can do way better than that!" Kierra voiced, giving him an unyielding gaze. "What'chu got low self-esteem or some shit? That bitch pussy and head that good?" Kierra pried.

"Maan you tripping," Face stated.

"N'all, nigga you tripping! I bet'chu can't name one thang y'all got in common outside of sex."

"Tss…!" Face exhaled.

"And you got the audacity to be round here killin' niggas over that old garbage ass hoe."

"What?"

"Don't play stupid. Everybody know wassup, Face. Look, I ain't tryna break ya down or nothing like that. I'm just tryna help you realize that you a different type of nigga. You supposed to be with a real bad azz solid bitch! Not no street walking prostitute. That shit got me pissed off, Face," Kierra proclaimed.

Face laid in silence but knew Kierra was giving it to him blood raw.

"I'm get off that kuz I got more important shit going on that I wanna talk to you about."

Kierra grabbed Face's chin and turned his face towards hers.

"Face, I got Cancer," she revealed.

"What?" He implored constriction in his voice.

"Yeah, my side was hurting me real bad. I went to the doctor, and he told me I got cancer on my ovaries. I'm doing chemo though," Kierra informed calmly as if she'd just told him she had a common cold.

"Damn," Face remarked, grabbing and pulling her closer. "You ready for what comes next?"

"I am," she retorted sternly. "If chemo fails, I'm prepared to die. Can't die but once," Kierra added her voice sharp.

"You a real gangsta. I admire yo' chi," Face asserted.

"My what?"

"Your energy."

Before Face could elaborate more, his phone rang.

"Yeah, was popping?" Face answered.

"Bra, what the fuck you done did?" World asked.

"What'chu mean?"

"Nigga, I just rode pass your spot and seen KoKo talking to them Krakaz.

"N'all?"

"Yeah bra. Look like she writing a whole novel and shit," he clowned.

"Damn! My money and my work over there. Brah, go get my whip and my money and shit," Face exclaimed.

"Nigga, I'm not fucking with that police ass hoe! You shoulda had your money tucked somewhere else. And your whip is fucked up. She done bust the windows and flattened the tires. I told you about fuckin with them rachet ass bitches!" World preached.

"I'on wanna hear that shit!"

Click! Face hung up the phone.

"You aight?" Kierra asked concerned.

"Hell nawl," Face retorted, calling the bondsman.

After talking to the bondsman, he found out that he had felonies. Kidnapping False Imprisonment, Aggravated

Assault with a firearm and Possession of a firearm by convicted felon.

His bond was set at a ransom of $100,000. Face laid back in the bed, exhaled deeply and rubbed his hand over his face in frustration. Even though he has some serious charges against him, he was elated that KoKo hadn't told about the murders she'd witnessed.

"KoKo got'chu in some shit, huh?" Kierra inquired.

"Yeah, she got me crossed up," he admitted.

"So, you gon' still fuck wit this hoe after she called the law on you?"

"Shid, I'on know," Face retorted, shrugging his shoulders.

"You real deal love that hoe," Kierra voiced in disgust.

"Yeah, I love the bitch. I'm fucked up about her. The only reason she called them krakaz on me is because I didn't come home last night," Face defended.

Kierra gazed at Face ambivalently. She had love for him, hated him, and felt sorry for him simultaneously.

"You making excuses for this police as hoe? She must of blew all in your ass and shit."

"Wat'cha mouth!" Warned Face.

"That's how you acting! You real tender as fuck!" Kierra snapped.

"Whateva," Face, retorted dialing a number.

"Ummm…what the fuck you calling my phone for?"

Click!

KoKo hung the phone up on Face. He called back and she picked up on the third ring.

"What?" KoKo answered.

"Damn, bae, why you tripping?" Face asked in a storm of confusion and pain.

"Why is you calling me? Ain't'chu wit'cha lil bitch?" KoKo inquired with a supercilious attitude.

"Maaan, why you put all them charges on me?" Face implored.

Moments ticked by with no reply from KoKo.

"All I wanted to do was come home and tell you how much I love you. When I seen you talking to them Krakaz," Face lied.

"Who is she, Face?"

Feeling sick to her stomach, Kierra got out of bed to go take a shower.

"Remember Meka? The bitch you fought in the club?"

"What about her?"

"That's her daughter. I used to fuck her mama, so she was like a daughter to me. That's it, bae," Face lied again.

"Yeah, you prolly put that dick on that lil hoe too. Where you at?"

"I been with my lil brother all night. We parked at a restaurant finna grab some shit to eat," Face continued to lie.

"Oh, you with World? Kuz I was sholl was lookin for your ass all night. I been up all night crying and shit," KoKo admitted.

"I'm sorry, bae. You know a nigga love you. You know exactly how I'm coming bout'chu," Face genuinely stated.

"I love you too daddy, and I'ma get them charges dropped."

"I need you," cried Face.

"I need you too, daddy."

"Look, I'm finna go get a room, I'm text you the room number."

"Okay daddy," KoKo retorted excitedly.

"When you come, bring that work and my money. My phone been blowing up for that work."

"I got'chu daddy," she assured.

"Love you."

"Love you too, daddy." *Click.*

When Face hung up the phone, Kierra was standing next to the bed, gazing at him in disbelief.

"You really finna go back to that hoe?'

"I got to. She got my work and like 30 rocks at the spot."

"You keep all that in one spot? With her knowing. Tsss…
You gone learn fatally," Kierra pronounced.

Chapter 22
Man Down

Slurping sounds echoed throughout the motel room from the ferocious head KoKo was administering to Face. His ass cheeks clenched tight while he gripped the sheets and fought to keep KoKo from sucking the soul from his body.

"Fffffuck!" Face yelled through clenched teeth as his legs trembled.

"Ummm...Ummm...Ummhmm!" KoKo moaned bobbing, twisting, and turning her head proficiently.

"Sss...Sshit, I'm finna..."

Before Face could finish his statement, KoKo snatched his dick out of her mouth and straddled him. She placed her hands on his chest, leaned forward, and proceeded to bounce on his dick rapidly. Face gazed at the mirror in front of the bed and watched KoKo velvet soft ass cheeks bounce poetically. The very sight of it caused Face to explode deep inside her warm, wet pussy. KoKo came in tandem then climbed off to clean him with her mouth.

"Damn, bae. You a fuckin animal!" Face declared, chasing his breath.

"Umm...I'm your animal daddy," she retorted, crawling up Face's body and kissing him on the lips.

She then laid beside him and caressed his chest tenderly.

"I love you, KoKo."

"I love you too, daddy."

"Then why the fuck you call them Krakaz on me and put them charges on me?" He inquired somberly.

"I'm sorry daddy. I just thought that you was gone leave me for that lil young bitch. She so much prettier, and that lil hoe had a nice ass body. I didn't wanna lose you, daddy, so I panicked. I promise you I'm have them charges dropped daddy," KoKo lamented.

"You know damn well another bitch could never take your place. I'm out here killing niggaz bout'chu and you think I'll leave you for a lil young hoe? Come on nah. You know better than that."

"You right daddy, I'm sorry."

"It's aight. You got my work and paper?"

"Of course, daddy. Let me use the bathroom right quick, then I'ma go get it out the car," KoKo stated, grabbing her clothes and heading to the restroom.

Face grabbed a half of blunt and put flame to it. He took a few hits and gazed at the ceiling while his thoughts rampant. Moments later, KoKo emerged from the bathroom and headed for the door.

"Give me a second daddy. I'm finna grab your stuff," she proclaimed before walking out the door.

Several minutes passed by when Face thought he heard noises that resembled walkie-talkies.

"Da fuck?" He muttered before sitting up.

Seconds later, several undercovers and U.S. Marshalls entered the room with weapons drawn.

"King! Don't fucking move!" A Marshall yelled, pointing his M-16 in Face's face.

"Maan, let me out some clothes on," Face asked,

"Go ahead," a detective told him.

Face removed the covers, revealing his nakedness to the gang. He then grabbed his clothes from the floor and got dressed. A Marshall then placed cuffs on his wrists and read him his rights. When Face stepped outside, KoKo rushed him and hugged him.

"I love you daddy," she stated, kissing Face on the lips.

"I love you too," he retorted.

After being placed in the undercover car, the detective turned in his seat to speak to Face.

"How old are you?'

"Twenty-two," Face answered.

"Aw, shit," the detective retorted, putting the car in drive and pulling off.

The detective knew the charges wouldn't stick. How could his victim be in danger to his suspect if they were caught together in a motel? She'd just hugged and kissed him in front of authorities. He knew there would be no cooperation on her behalf.

***

Due to Face's criminal history, he was placed in Delta. Delta was where the high-risk inmates were housed. It held six inmates to a room behind a door. There was no sunshine, even at recreation. Face entered the cell. It was a little after six o'clock. Four inmates were up telling war stories while one remained under the cover appearing to be sleep.

"Wassup my nigga?" A youngin named Man Man implored.

"Wass popping?" Face retorted, throwing his mat in his bunk.

"I'm Man Man from da 3," he stated proudly.

"Oh, you from 23rd? I fuck wit da 3," Face added.

"I'm German Boy, 13th Street," another inmate chimed in.

"Quan from the projects."

"Boot, 23rd."

"I'm Face, Blood Gang," he stated arrogantly.

Upon hearing that the inmate who was under the cover peeked his head out.

"Face?"

"B3?" Face cantered.

"Mane, this shit crazy mane!" B3 added jumping out of his rack to show Face some love.

They dapped each other up and smiled happy to see each other.

"Mane, I ain't seen you since we stomped that nigga out at the Elks, mane."

Face laughed at the memory.

"Why you in here?" Face asked.

"That goddamn child support, mane. I'll be out in a few weeks, mane."

"They got'chu in Delta for child support?"

"I got a long history mane. But shid why you in here, mane?"

"Bitch done put all kinda charges on me," Face admitted.

"KoKo?"

"Yeah, man."

"Mane, I told you, mane! I told you, KoKo was gone take you up through there, mane!"

"KoKo?" German Boy questioned.

"Yeah," Face answered, eagerly moving closer to German boy.

"KoKo from the 3? She like twenty-six with a fie ass body and a stank walk?"

"Yeah, that's her," Face assured.

"Oh, that's that baby! She a real thot type, animalistic type bitch, but boy… that's that baby! Shid, the night before last, I had that thick shit folded up, killing that pussy! My lil nigga came in behind me and trained that hoe! Good pussy!" German Boy enunciated.

B3 looked at Face while Face realized that was the same night KoKo left him at Wal-Mart.

Crack! Face hit German boy in the chin, dropping him instantly. Out of pure instinct, B3 jumped in helping Face stomp on his head.

"Y'all boyz chill! Y'all gone kill him," Man Man warned.

Face grabbed B3 by his shirt and pulled him back. When he looked at German Boy, he realized that he was having a seizure. Face walked by the door and pressed the intercom button.

"Yeah?" The C.O. answered.

"Man down!" Face exclaimed.

Moments later, the ASAP team rushed in the room.

"What the fuck happened?"

"He having a seizure. He just fell outta his rack and bust his face up," Face stated.

An officer turned German Boy on his side until the seizure subsided. When he was conscious they took him out to medical.

Chapter 23
Run Ya Mouth

World was in One Stop Shop's corner store with two of his Blood homies buying blunts and scratch off tickets.

"Aye, wassup? Y'all niggaz wanna fall in the club tonight?" Bloody J asked.

"Hell yeah!" EJ added.

"Maaan, hell nawl! I'm trapping all night," World asserted, paying the owner of the store before grabbing his blunts and scratch offs to leave.

"You can trap at the club, Blood. Somebody always need weed in the club," Bloody J declared, following World out of the store with EJ behind.

"I'm not going. Y'all niggas waste ya re-up money while I'ma be chewing," World declared, walking past a car that looked familiar.

"You geeking, homie," EJ added.

"Da fuck?" World quipped looking into a car that was parked next to his. "Bitch! I know you ain't got another nigga driving my brother shit!"

"It ain't even like that! This my kuz…" KoKo words were cut short when World spit in her face.

"Pussy ass hoe!" World snapped.

Before she could wipe the spit from her face, the youngin who was driving Face's car boldly stepped out.

"Maaan, you gotta nigga fucked up," Knight stated while clutching.

"Oh, you clutching?" Bloody J inquired reaching for his strap.

Boc! Boc! Boc!

Knight upped and squeezed three shots off hitting Bloody J in the head and EJ in the shoulder. World snatched out and fired wildly, missing Knight who had ducked behind Face's car and returned fire. KoKo ducked and jumped into the backseat as bullets tore through the car miraculously missing her. EJ managed to get a hold of his weapon and fired aimlessly, missing Knight. When World rose from behind his car, he seen Knight running low, slipping between cars making a run for it. World fired a few more shots then hopped in his car.

"EJ, come on nigga!" World yelled, starting the car.

"We can't leave Bloody J!" EJ cried.

"That nigga dead! Let's go!"

EJ hopped in the car with World, and they left the scene with one less than they came.

***

35 days later…

Face had made a big goulash and shared it amongst his cellmates. He even gave German Boy a portion, who was now back from medical and had apologized profusely.

"I appreciate chu, bra," German boy asserted.

"You good, my nigga," Face retorted glancing at German Boy then diverting his attention back to the pictures KoKo had sent him of her tattooing Face's name on her neck.

The very thought of branding her with his name gave him an acute sense of empowerment. Unbeknownst to Face, the same night KoKo got the tattoo, she also gave the tattooist a slice of pussy.

"Damn, mane! KoKo been holding you down, mane. I know she the one put'chu in here, mane, but she holding shit down. Post cards, money on the phone, money on ya books, mane," B3 voiced

Face shook his head from right to left. "Shid, it's my money, Face cantered.

"Still, mane. She didn't have to send you shit, mane. The KoKo I know woulda just clean ran off, mane," B3 proclaimed, stuffing food in his mouth.

"Hell yeah," Man Man added.

All this talk about KoKo was making Face miss her profoundly. All day everyday flashbacks of her fie head and pussy combo pervaded his mental. It was as if the power of her pussy was haunting him day in day out.

"I'll be back," Face pronounced, leaving out of the cell to go use the phone.

He spotted one that was available, grabbed it, and quickly dialed KoKo's number.

To his surprise, it went straight to voicemail. Face tried again and got the same results. The third time the phone just continued to ring with no answer. Face's heart rate increased as he stood at the phone and called several more times with no answer. He finally decided to say fuck it and returned to his cell, conflicted and drained. He hopped in his rack and pulled the covers over his head.

"Wassup mane? You aight?" B3 asked concerned.

"Yeah, I'm good," Face lied.

"Just checking, mane."

"Fasho. I'ma fuck wit'chu tomorrow," Face retorted.

"Love," B3 added.

After doing bid after bid, everybody in the room could tell when somebody had a bad phone call or no call at all. Knowing how violent Face was, nobody dared to ask him about it. For the next three days, Face got the same results when trying to contact KoKo. Her failure to communicate led him to believe that she was going to cooperate with the state. He's lost his sense of taste, barely eating or sleeping and didn't know if he was coming or going.

After pacing back and forth on the top tier for nearly an hour, Face decided to try his luck and called his last five minutes before lockdown.

When KoKo finally answered, he didn't know what to say or do.

"Wassup?" KoKo answered cockily.

Shocked at her tone, Face just sat in silence.

"What? Wassup? You been blowing up my phone for days, nah you ain't got nothin to say? Run ya mouth!" She yelled, snuffling a chuckle.

"Why the fuck you ain't been picking up the phone?" Face inquired, fearing the answer.

"I found somebody," she answered with no empathy.

Face heart fell to his nuts as his pressure rose.

"Fuck you mean, you found somebody?"

Face could hear a man's voice in the background telling KoKo to hang up the phone.

Click!

KoKo hung up on Face with no conscious. The sound of KoKo hanging up on him at another man's command left Face enervated He managed to drag himself to his cell to bury his wounded flesh under his blanket. It baffled him that KoKo could tattoo his name and break up with him in the same week. Face was so distraught that he thought he'd succumb from heartbreak.

Two days later, Face's name rang over the intercom for him to pack up. It had been 40 days without the state picking up the charges, so they were dropped. Face left everything to B3 and headed to booking.

Chapter 24
You Trippin'

Face didn't want Kierra, Siearra, or World to patronize him with I told you so, so he called Quanda to come get him which she happily obliged. She took him by his spot on 25th Street to pick up whatever he had left, but when he tried his key, it didn't work. He peeked inside and seen that the apartment was completely empty.

"I'ma kill this bitch," Face muttered on his way back to Quanda's truck. He hopped inside with rage obvious in his manner.

"Wass wrong, baby?" Quanda implored.

"This bitch dun ran off with my money and work. The whole fucking apartment is empty."

"Damn, that's real flaw shit. You, umm…want me to take you somewhere? You hungry or anything?" She offered.

"I don't want nobody to know I'm out right nah," Face retorted.

"You can come to my house. I stay in a gated community. It's real chillax out there. No hood niggaz or thots," Quanda pitched.

"Yeah, I'ma go to your spot," Face agreed.

***

"Oooow, ffffuck yeah! Sss, ride that dick, Quanda," Quanda coached herself as she rode Face by the kitchen table in a chair reverse cowgirl.

Face just sat there inactive as she rode him crazy. His mind was to cluttered with thought of his money, work, and KoKo. Most importantly, he wanted to know who the nigga was most likely spending his money.

"Ffffuck, I'm cummin' baby! Ooow, I'm cuming on this dick," Quanda cried switching from a bouncing motion to a hard grind.

Face found himself cuming with her as she constricted her walls around him and became extremely wetter.

"Ffffffuck! That was so good," Quanda declared, kissing Face's dick before leaving to grab baby wipes.

When she returned, Face was on the phone arguing.

"Nigga, put my bitch on the phone, pussy ass nigga!" Face demanded.

"That's my bitch, nah! Find you another one," Knight cantered.

"Just let me talk to her!" Face pleaded.

"Bra, look how you actin about this hoe. Keep it playa and find you another one, my nigga," Knight clowned. *Click!*

Pain fanned throughout Face's body vehemently.

"You gone be aight," Quanda assured wiping Face's dick clean with the baby wipes.

He inhaled and exhaled deeply rubbing his hands across his face in frustration. Quanda left for a brief moment then returned.

"Here Face," she said sitting ten racks on the table. "Look, I know we're not together, and I'm not trying to pressure you into being with me. I'm just tryna sho' you that'chu better than that and you don't need her to make you feel whole. You don't need her, Face. She don't deserve your energy or your inner G. I dun seen what'chu capable of, and I believe in you. Take this money and power back up. I'll get mines on the back end, no pressure," Quanda enunciated beautifully.

Face glanced at the money and then gazed at Quanda in adulation. It baffled him that this woman who barely knew him believed in him enough to give him probably her life's savings to generate motion again.

"You sho?" Face inquired.

"I'm more than positive, baby," Quanda said, placing a kiss on Face's lips.

Face stood up, grabbed the money and spread it over the kitchen table. He then lifted Quanda, placed her on top of the money and fucked her into a blissful submission.

***

The next morning, Face pulled up to his mother's house where Moses was waiting on him. Quanda had given him her truck to handle his business with no rush. Face hopped out of the truck and approach Moses who was posted in the driveway smoking a blunt.

"Wass popping, bra?' Face greeted, dapping Moses up.

"Wass hadnin?" Moses retorted, passing Face the blunt.

He took a pull, inhaled deeply then blew smoke from his nose. "Bra, look. I know you heard about what happened. Pussy ass hoe put them fake ass charges on me and ran off with my money and work. I got ten bands that I scraped up out the streets. I need you to fuck with me bra, and I'll clean my face on what I owe you, my nigga," Face promised hitting the blunt again before passing it back to Moses.

"That lil shit girl ran off with, don't even trip off that. Just give me them ten and I'm turn you all the way up. Nah, I know you love girl or whateva, and I'll neva tell a man where his heart should be, but I will tell you this… just be careful bra. You know what type of broad you dealing with nah. She dun showed you… nah believe her."

"Respect," Face cantered.

"So, what'chu gone do about that lil beef situation, kuz money don't mix with war.

"What beef?" Face implored.

"Oh, you don't know? Well, I'ma let'cha brother tell you. He in there. Let me get them ten, and I'm pull back up in like an hour," Moses pronounced.

Face handed Moses the ten racks then headed inside looking for World. Before he could find World, he ran into his mother, Pandora in the kitchen.

"Wassup Mama," Face greeted, hugging and kissing her on the neck.

"Hey son, you doing alright?" She asked, putting her hands on her lap.

"Yeah, ma I'm good."

"So, you dun found one who pit'chu in jail, and take ya money huh?"

"Come on, ma," Face retorted.

"I ain't gone preach to you. If you like it, I love it. But don't expect me to come visit no jail house, kuz I ain't. Nah, I love you, but I just can't do it. Not behind no skeezer. I'm finna run to the store, you need anything?" Pandora offered.

"N'all ma. I'm good and I love you too."

"Okay, see ya later," she asserted before leaving through the garage.

Face slid to the back room and found World smoking a blunt and counting money with a baby arsenal in front of him.

"Wass popping?" Face greeted locking Bs with World.

"Niggas like us," World retorted.

"What this beef shit about, Moses speaking on?' Face asked taking a seat next to World on the couch.

World sat the money on the table and gave Face the spill.

"Bra when you was in lock, I came out the store with Blood J and EJ right. How about I view another nigga in the driver seat of your whip with KoKo on the passenger."

Face's blood started to boil instantly.

"So, you know me, I snapped and spit in the hoe face. The nigga, hop out your shit and go to hitting off the rip. He hit Blood J in the head and EJ in the shoulder. The nigga caught me off guard when he started hitting out the gate. I fumbled with my strap but managed to get it out and started hitting back. EJ was hitting too, but the bitch ass nigga got away."

Face took in everything and shook his head up and down.

"Okay," Face added in a calm but threating tone. "So, kuz dead?"

"Yeah, Bloody J gone bra," World informed.

"Where EJ?"

"His mama put him on the first thing smoking back to Kentucky."

"KoKo?"

"She ain't get hit. That shit brazy, fool. The whip had holes in it. I'on view how she made it," World proclaimed.

"Who the nigga she was with?"

"I just found out it's a nigga named Knight," World announced.

Face rubbed his chin in deep thought. "Just lay back and vibe. Get money bra. I got this shit," Face declared.

"Fuck you mean? This nigga killed fam. I'm on his top!" World snapped.

"N'all, lil bra. All this shit behind me and you just had a baby, fool. Lay back on this one. It'll be plenty more, nigga. Stand down."

World exhaled seething.

"You tripping," World voiced.

Chapter 25
Prove It

One month later, Face had powered back up. He paid Quanda back her money and used her A1 credit to sign for him a 2023 BMX 840i X, to drive straight off the lot. Instead of grabbing a home of his own, he stayed nights at Quanda's and days trapping out of his mother's garage. It was a Friday, dark and Face was closing down shop when a Ford Taurus pulled into the driveway, killing its lights. Face pulled his .40 with an extended 30 on it and approached the vehicle. When he got closer, he noticed that it was KoKo. He quickly scanned his surroundings before placing his attention back on KoKo.

"I'm not here to set'chu up, Face. I just need to talk to you," KoKo declared stepping out of the car in a tight-fitting Chanel dress that barely covered her ass and camel toe.

Her hair and nails were done to perfection making her a sight to see.

"We ain't got shit to talk about," Face stated, tucking his pistol in his Amiri's.

KoKo turned to reach in her car to grab her clutch, bending over making sure to give Face an eye full.

"I just wanted to tell you that I'm sorry for putting them charges on you, and that somebody seen you, and noticed you from the newspapers. It was a thousand-dollar bounty on your head, and somebody cashed it in, daddy. I also apologize for cheating on you, but that was just a fling. I don't love him. I don't love none of these niggaz but you, daddy. You the only nigga I ever gave my heart to. Them other niggaz was just a nut. And I'm sorry about your cousin, baby but that wasn't my fault," KoKo explained, reaching in her clutch.

"Here, daddy," she said, handing Face a stack of bills.

"I know you left close to thirty racks, but this is fifteen. I promise I'll get the rest of it, daddy," she promised.

"Where my work at?" Face implored calmly.

"He took it," she admitted.

Face took the money from her hands and tucked it. "We ain't got nothing else to talk about," he quipped.

KoKo quickly grabbed both of his hands and put one on her ass and one under the front of her dress. Her ass was so soft, and her pussy was so warm. Face's dick rose instantly.

"You sure we ain't got nothin to talk about?" KoKo inquired slipping her hands inside Face's Amiri's.

***

Smack! Smack! Smack! Smack! The sound of Face hitting KoKo from the back echoed throughout the room that she had been staying in at the Treasure Coast Inn. When Face was incarcerated, KoKo was hiding out at the Treasure Coast Inn from the detectives who wanted her to testify on Face. She had been staying there ever since and had became quite known amongst the place.

"Ooow! Fffuck, daddy! Ssss…Whooo, I miss you daddy! Ssss, whooo… ssshit, yes!" KoKo cried out loudly.

Moments later, there was aggressive knocking in the door.

"KoKo! KoKo, I know you in there! Open the door, bae. I'm sorry!" Knight pleaded.

Face stopped fucking KoKo.

"That's him?" He asked.

"Mm-huh," KoKo answered quickly.

Face could have easily opened the door and killed him, but he wanted to tug at his heart strings first. Face repositioned KoKo bending her over a table that sat in front of the room window.

"KoKo!" Knight called out now banging on the window directly in front of Face and KoKo.

Face snatched the curtains opened and began to fuck KoKo hard from the back. He made sure to long stroke her making her ass clap with every thrust while looking Knight in his eyes.

"No!" Knight yelled banging on the window. "KoKo, please!"

"Who pussy this is?" Face taunted.

"Whoo, ffffuck! Sss... this your pussy, daddy!"

Smack! Face slapped her ass aggressively.

"Say fuck that pussy nigga!" *Smack!*

"Fuck who?"

"Knight! Ssss...damn daddy! You in this pussy.... fffffuck!"

When Face felt his nut coming he snatched out, grabbed KoKo by her hair and forced her on her knees.

"No, bae, don't...do it! Please!" Knight cried as he watched Face nut all in KoKo's mouth.

Face bit his bottom lip while gazing into Knight's eyes. He could hear KoKo's slurping sounds through the window. Knight pulled his pistol from his hip and aimed it at the window. Face blew a kiss at him, taunting him more.

"Hey what the fuck are you doing motherfucker?" A concerned neighbor asked Knight.

Knight quickly tucked his pistol,

"I'm get'chu nigga! That's on gang!" Knight promised, banging on the window before leaving.

Face closed the curtain then got comfortable in the bed. He made KoKo go tell the neighbor that all was good while he fired up a blunt. When she came back, she snuggled under Face and caressed his flesh.

"Daddy, you crazy," KoKo said placing a kiss on his chest.

"So, what the bituation with you and fool?" Face questioned.

"Nothing daddy, I promise. I know when you was in jail, I told you I found somebody, but I had told him when you came home, me and him was over. I guess he is having a hard time letting go. I didn't even know you was home until my lil sister told me she had seen you wit that hoe Quanda. So, tell me. What's the bituation with you and her?"

"You love that nigga?" Face asked ignoring her question.

"Fuck no! I told you, you the only one whoever had my heart and still do daddy," KoKo expressed.

"Oh yeah?"

"Yeah, daddy."

"Prove it."

Chapter 26
Face

Face was sitting on the passenger seat of Quanda's truck parked in his mother's driveway smoking a blunt.

"Let me hit the blunt baby," Quanda asked.

Face took a pull then handed her the blunt. He then grabbed his phone and strolled down Facebook.

"Damn," Face cried as pain hit him in the impetus of a tidal wave.

"What? What happened, daddy?" Quanda asked.

Face lapsed into a simmering silence before answering Quanda's question.

"My homegirl died of cancer," Face answered as vivid memories of Kierra lurked in his consciousness.

"I'm sorry to hear that, baby," Quanda asserted, passing him the blunt and rubbing his back.

Face let his seat back and gazed at the roof of the truck. Quanda swiftly slipped Face's dick from his Bottega Vaneta joggers and placed it deep in her warm mouth.

"Mmmm," Face moaned while Quanda attempted to suck his pain away.

Before she could switch gears, there was a knock at Face's window. When he opened his eyes, he noted World standing on the other side of the 5% tent. He cracked the window.

"Wass popping?" Face implored.

"Maaaan, get'cho dick outta her mouth and step out bra. You tripping," World sputtered.

Face let the window back up.

"Pardon my soul for a minute ma," Face said to Quanda.

She pulled Face out of her mouth and wiped hers.

"Handle ya business, baby," she retorted.

Face stepped out of the truck and walked off with World.

"Wassup wit'chu bra?"

"What'chu mean, gang" Face replied, still smoking his blunt.

"It's been over a month! Nah, I dun did what you told me to do and fell back. I'on view no results. On top of that, while you caked up in the driveway getting ya dicked licked, I just seen that bitch ass nigga in traffic with that hoe KoKo! He lucky I left my strap but don't trip. I just wanted to let'chu know when I spot'em again, I got'em! On Gang, bra!" World voiced then walked inside, leaving Face standing in the driveway.

Face batted the air with his hand and hopped back in the truck with Quanda.

"You okay, baby?" Quanda implored.

"I'm always aight," he retorted then laid his seat back so that Quanda could finish administering brain anatomy.

***

It was a little after 10:30 p.m. when KoKo decided to pull up to the coke man's house in Lakewood Park. She needed a good amount that would last for at least two days.

"Who stay here, bae?" Knight asked. Him and KoKo had been back kicking it ever since Face decided to go back to Quanda. Despite KoKo allowing herself to be seen getting fucked by Face, Knight readily took her back. He was two years younger than Face, so KoKo had no problem opening his nose wide. Knight was beyond tender.

"The dope man. You want some Mollies?" She offered.

"Yeah, get me a gram, bae."

"Okay," KoKo retorted, attempting to open the door.

"Wait, bae," Knight pleaded.

"What?"

"Give me a kiss before you leave," Knight stated, licking his lips.

KoKo did her signature seductive laugh then kissed him tenderly. Knight slipped his hand under her mini skirt and tampered with her clit.

"Hmm," KoKo moaned, breaking away from their kiss and pulling Knight's dick out.

She wasted no time making his dick disappear over and over in her mouth.

"Ol... sssshit!" Knight yelled loudly in the quiet of the night.

Pop! KoKo popped his dick out of her mouth.

"Umm, um. You entirely too loud. We'll finish this later," KoKo declared making her exit.

"Bae, wait!" Knight pleaded.

"Shh," KoKo advised putting her index finger over her closed lipped smile as she paused in front of her car and headed to the side door where everyone got served.

"Damn, that bitch can suck a dick," Knight muttered pulling a Newport from his pack and adding flame to it.

"Wass poppin' gang?"

Boc! Boc! Boc!

Three Boattail Frangible rounds pierced Knight's midsection. Boattail Frangible are lead free bullets that break up into small pieces on contact. Knight clutched his midsection before glancing up at the hooded figure. Face took his hood off long enough for Knight to recognize who he was then pulled it back over his head. Knight jumped into the driver's side and opened the door hitting the ground running.

Boc! Boc!

Two more rounds tore his back up as he fell in the neighbor's yard and began to crawl toward their door. He looked back and seen Face standing over him.

"Help! Somebody help! He gone kill me!" Knight yelled from his fading soul.

Knight managed to make it to the door and banges on it for dear life.

"Help me, please!"

The door swung open, and an old lady saw Knight bleeding profusely.

"He trying to kill me," he screamed, turning around only to find Face gone.

"Oh, dear Lord, Hold on baby while I call the ambulance,"

The old lady called the ambulance and when they arrived, Knight was barely alive.

"Talk to me, what happened?" A medic asked, preparing to put him on a stretcher.

"Face," Knight muttered.

"What?"

"Face did it," Knight stated with the last breath in his body.

He flatlined before he could make it to the ambulance. KoKo never came out of the dopeman's house on the account that she helped facilitate his demise. Face and KoKo planned Knight's murder that same night at the motel. Face had put a tracker on KoKo's car and was patiently waiting to catch him by total surprise.

Chapter 27
Hood Ink

There had been whispers of Knight being seen with KoKo, but nothing prosecutorial ever came of it. People who knew that Knight and KoKo were intimate looked at her disdainfully in public because everyone knew that Face would kill for her love. After the murder, Face had convinced KoKo to sell her car in exchange for his Mercury. They were now officially back together and known around the city as the most toxic couple in existence. In Face's twisted thinking, KoKo's facilitation in the murder proved her loyalty to him and he wanted to signify his gratitude.

"Welcome to Hood Ink, my nigga!" Arkbar, the owner of the tattoo shop greeted.

"This ain't my first trip here, my nigga, knock it off," Face retorted, smiling from ear to ear and dapping Arkbar up.

"I know, I just like how that shit sound, my nigga."

"I hear you, was popping though?" Face cantered.

"Chasin this mothafucking money, nigga," Arkbar retorted.

"Mandatory! Peep, game though. I'm tryna get wet up."

"Fasho, my nigga. What'chu tryna get?"

KoKo walked in and kissed Face.

"Hey Arkbar," KoKo spoke.

"Wassup, girl?"

"Chillin up here with my man," she stated, excitedly smiling.

"That's what I'm tryna get. I want her name across the front of my neck," Face declared.

"That shit going be hard as fuck, my nigga! I just got my girl name tatted," Arkbar informed, showing Face his neck tattoo. "But check it though. I gotta client on the way, so I'ma let my lil brother ink you up. Don't trip, he gas, my nigga. Bra get'em right," Arkbar commanded.

"Wass popping, my nigga? I'm Miami," Arkbar's little brother greeted.

"You homie?" Face questioned.

"TTP 400 Westside," Miami stated proudly.

"Billy Gang, Eastside. Wass popping?" Face retorted bumping Bs with Miami.

"Who your big fool is?"

"Kream," Face stated.

"I know fool. He in the feds right?"

"Yeah."

"What'chu want again?"

"KoKo across the front of my neck."

"Aight, I got'chu. Let me setup right quick," Miami proclaimed, getting his tools ready.

"Arkbar, I'm allowed to roll up in here?" Asked Face.

"As long as you got that good coke in it, my nigga," Arkbar pronounced.

"Say none," Face asserted, rolling up two dirty blunts.

He handed Arkbar one and then fired his up.

"Let's do it, my nigga," Miami insisted.

"I love you daddy," KoKo said kissing Face before he laid in the tattoo chair.

"Love you more."

KoKo stood and took bumps of coke while watching Face brand her name. Twenty minutes later, Miami was done.

"You good, my nigga," Miami assured handing Face a mirror.

"Yeah, that bitch hard!" Face admitted.

"Them hoes ain't gone like that," KoKo added, taking another bump.

"Them niggaz ain't neither," Face cantered, rising from the chair.

"Here daddy," KoKo said putting a bump of coke to Face nose.

He took a bump on each side then thanked Miami for his work.

"I'm finna go start the car, daddy," KoKo declared, leaving out of the shop.

"I'm a fuck wit'chu, Arkbar," Face proclaimed dapping Arkbar before leaving.

"Fasho, my nigga!" Arkbar replied.

Face left out of the room and headed to the door. He opened it then patted his pocket, realizing he left his Newports in the shop. He closed the door back and patted his pockets again.

"That nigga a real sucka, my nigga," Miami expressed.

Face's face crinkled and thought that he had heard wrong. He tiptoed to the edge of the wall and eavesdropped.

"Don't do that, bra. That's his bitch, my nigga," Arkbar retorted.

"Bra, when this nigga was locked up, she came to me and got his named tatted on her neck. The same night, she gave me the pussy. The hoe swallow and all! Straight animal and she break bread, my nigga."

"You sho you ain't mad that she ain't fuckin wit'chu no moe?" Arkbar implored.

"You tripping! That hoe was fucking me and Knight, my nigga. And she knew that was my homie. Straight slut, my nigga. I know that he prolly set my dog up, my nigga!" Miami voiced.

"Maan you trippin'. I'm finna take me a shit before my client pull up," Arkbar stated before sliding into the restroom.

Anguish and murderous thoughts besieged Face's mind, body, and soul. If Miami would have pulled Face to the side, he would have still been in his feelings but would have handled the situation in a different manner. Face drew his pistol and rounded the wall squeezing off shots.

Boc! Boc! Boc! Boc! Boc! Boc!

Face planted five in Miami hitting him in the face, neck, and chest dropping him and blood all over his tattoo equipment. Face slipped out the door unseen and hopped into his BMW's passenger side.

"Go!" Face yelled.

KoKo followed the command instantly.

"What happened daddy," KoKo inquired her adrenaline and pussy juices pumping.

"That bitch ass nigga Miami thought I was gone, and I heard him telling Arkbar that you set Knight up. And he was calling you all kinda sluts and hoes and shit. You already know I gave it to him.

"Arkbar?"

"He was in the bathroom. He ain't see shit," Face explained, taking a bump of coke.

KoKo was silent for a moment, then spoke her mind. "That's what that pussy nigga get!" KoKo voiced. "Give me kiss daddy."

Face leaned over and kissed her.

"I love you, daddy."

"A nigga love you too.

Chapter 28
On Gang!

Miami's murder had the fuzz combing the city for any type of leads. The homicide detectives questioned Arkbar but he kept it solid and told them that he was in the restroom and heard what sounded like a robbery. Days after the murder, he opened the shop back up and resumed back to business. Nothing never came of Knight's confession to the medic because Face wasn't Face real name. It was Fatief King.

After laying low for a week, Face gave KoKo the money to get a home in Sunland Garden. They were snuggled up watching Young Wild and Free while smoking a blunt of Panama Haze.

"Bae," KoKo asserted turning the TV down.

"Wassup bae, you tripping! Turn it back up," Face pronounced.

"You know they said Knight gave the paramedics your name, right?"

"Yeah. That bitch ass nigga turned rat before he died. I ain't tripping off that shit though," Face retorted, swiping the air with his hand in dismissal.

"I was just telling you, daddy," she added concerned.

"They ain't got nothing. Nah, please turn the TV back up," he pleaded, hitting the blunt.

KoKo turned the volume back up then grabbed her phone to stroll Facebook. Out of Face's peripheral, he noted

KoKo's expression as she brought the phone closer to her face for proper viewing but didn't pay it any real attention. KoKo climbed out of bed and appeared to be sending a text. Face's phone vibrated. He looked over to grab his phone and seen that he had a message.

"Da fuck?" Face implored seeing that he had a message from KoKo.

"Why the fuck you sent me a text if you right here?" Face asked, never looking up from his phone.

He opened the message. By the time he looked up, KoKo was on his ass.

Crack! She hit Face in the bridge of his nose, splitting him instantly.

"Pussy ass nigga!" KoKo snapped, hitting him a few more times across the head before running to the kitchen to get a knife.

KoKo had sent Face a screenshot of him and Quanda laid up in bed. Quanda had tagged Face in the picture being messy. She was acting maliciously with a broken heart knowing that KoKo would see it and act on it.

"Bae, that picture old!" Face pleaded attempting to stop the bleeding from the split in his nose.

KoKo rushed back into the room with the knife.

"The date is on the fuckin picture, stupid ass nigga!"

The date on the photo showed that the picture was taken the day before Knight's murder.

"Bae, you tripping! That hoe don't mean nothin to me! I just tatted yo name cross my throat. I'm with who I love!" Face continued.

"I wouldn't give no fucks! Get the fuck out!" KoKo yelled in tears.

"Bitch, I paid for this house! You got me fucked up!"

"Leave or I'ma call them Krakaz!" She threatened.

"You a real police ass hoe!" Face stated, putting on his clothes.

"Sholl is! Nah leave or I'm a tell them Krakaz wassup!"

Face gazed at KoKo ambivalently then grabbed his keys and left quietly.

***

It had been a week since Face's fight with KoKo and police or not, he missed her arduously. She had the ability to take his breath away and breathe life into him at the same time. In Face's mind, life was meaningless without her. He was now at war with World and Sierra drinking his pain away.

"My nigga, I like the way you handle that bidness, and stepped on lil buddy, but I'on like how you let that hoe treat'chu all kinda ways. You way to playa for that bra," World enunciated.

"For real! All these bitches out here, and you want a slut!" Sierra added.

"I like nasty, stanking, ratchet, slut bitches!" Face clowned, taking a shot of Patron to the face.

Sierra shook her head in disgust.

"That whore gone be the death of you," Sierra pronounced seriously.

"I was born by the pussy, die by the pussy!" Face continued to clown, quoting Chris Tucker in the movie *Dead Presidents*.

"Aight, nigga," World added.

"Man I'ma fuck wit y'all later," Face declared, standing and stumbling.

"You aight," Sierra asked.

"Yeah, I'm good," Face assured, stumbling out of the bar and hopping into his BMW.

Twenty minutes later, he managed to make it to Sunland Garden and pulled into the house that he had purchased for him and KoKo. He got out, stumbled to the door and attempted to use his key. After trying for ten minutes, he realized that the locks had been changed.

"This stupid ass bitch," Face slurred then made his way to the side of the house and climbed through their room window.

Face was so intoxicated that he flopped down on the bed and passed out. Thirty minutes later, KoKo came home with company and found Face passed out on their bed. Instead of waking him up, she called the police and told them that she had broken up with him, kicked him out and now he had broken into her house. When the police arrived, they found Face still asleep in bed lying on his back.

"King!" A cop yelled!

Face didn't move.

"Mr. King!" He yelled again kicking Face's foot that hung off the bed.

When Face opened his eyes, he seen that he was surrounded by cops pointing guns at him.

"Da fuck?" He spat, noting KoKo and a familiar face standing next to her.

"You're under arrest for Breaking and Entering! Get the fuck up slowly!"

Face put his hands in the air and slipped out of bed slowly all while watching KoKo with murder in his eyes. When he stood up, cuffs was placed on his wrists behind his back. An officer patted him down.

"Well, looky here, looky here! We gotta zero!" The officer stated excitedly referring to the gun that he's found on Face.

"Breaking and Entering, and Possession of a Firearm by a Convicted Felon," the officer enunciated proudly.

The whole time the officer was talking Face never took his eyes off of KoKo who bore a serpentine smirk on her face. The officers told KoKo to clear a path and she quickly headed outside with her company. When Face was brought outside, he noticed the nigga who was standing next to KoKo. Face knew him from around the way.

"Wass popping, Pooh Bear?" Face implored with a devilish smirk on his face.

Pooh Bear remained silent. He knew how Face got down.

"Hoe, I'ma kill you! On Gang, bitch, I'ma kill you!" Face promised.

"Umm hmm! Whateva, nigga!" KoKo retorted before Face was placed into the vehicle.

Chapter 29

Aaaahaaa!

Two days later, Face had posted bail on a fifty-thousand-dollar bond and was backed in at Golden Corral real fish-scale in a baser's rental. He'd been in the parking lot for over an hour with no appetite or intent of going in. Face took two bumps of coke then finally set eyes on what he'd been patiently waiting for. KoKo and Pooh Bear sauntered out of Golden Corral entangled, dripping with lascivious.

"Ooow, I gotcha ass, nah," Face muttered to himself grabbing two XD Springfield 45's

KoKo and Pooh Bear headed to Face's BMW jovially unaware of their surroundings and got in his car. Face hopped out bare face and made his way towards them from a blindside. When he stepped in front of his vehicle, KoKo and Pooh bear were lip-locking like lost lovers.

"Wass popping, Gang?" Face yelled.

KoKo and Pooh Bear broke away at the same time and diverted their attention through the windshield. Both of their eyes doubled in sized when they noted Face in front of the car smiling with virulence.

"Didn't I muthafuckin tell ya!" Face stated in his best impression of Bernie Mac before letting both pistols go.

Boc! Boc! Boc! Boc! Boc! Boc! Boc! Boc! Boc! Boc! Boc! Boc! Boc! Boc! Boc! Boc! Boc! Boc! Boc! Boc!

After letting off twenty rounds, Face left them both slumped and jetted back to his rented vehicle. He mashed the gas and attempted to pull out of the parking lot without looking both ways.

Bam! A F-350 hit Face in the left rear, spinning his vehicle.

By the time he' stopped spinning, he had been hit by three cars. Adrenaline pumping, he hopped out and car jacked the nearest vehicle. The mother was pulled out of the car while two kids were still in the backseat, High off coke, Face managed to hit another vehicle. The impact caused him to hit his head on the steering wheel, knocking him out. When Face came to he was surrounded by .40's, and M-16's. Face knew that he was done for and surrendered peacefully. He stepped out of the damaged vehicle with his hands up.

"Aaaahaa!" Face taunted, blowing a kiss at the government's gang.

***

A year later Face sat in Fort Pierce's cold Federal court room in a Saint Laurent suit next to his attorney stolidly. He had been offered a plea of 80 years, but he turned it down and sent word by his attorney that he wanted to suit up for trial. The day had finally arrived, and Face was fearless and numb to it all. Nothing could ever hurt him more than KoKo's betrayal.

"Your Honor! I'd like to call our first witness to the stand! Ullessia Bryant!" Stated the prosecutor insolently.

KoKo appeared from a side door and sauntered to the witness stand anxiously. Once seated, she gazed at Face smirking. She then raised her right hand and winked at Face.

Lock Down Publications and Ca$h Presents
Assisted Publishing Packages

BASIC PACKAGE	UPGRADED PACKAGE
$499	$800
Editing	Typing
Cover Design	Editing
Formatting	Cover Design
	Formatting
ADVANCE PACKAGE	**LDP SUPREME PACKAGE**
$1,200	$1,500
Typing	Typing
Editing	Editing
Cover Design	Cover Design
Formatting	Formatting
Copyright registration	Copyright registration
Proofreading	Proofreading
Upload book to Amazon	Set up Amazon account
	Upload book to Amazon
	Advertise on LDP, Amazon and Facebook Page

***Other services available upon request.
Additional charges may apply

Lock Down Publications
P.O. Box 944
Stockbridge, GA 30281-9998
Phone: 470 303-9761

Submission Guideline

Submit the first three chapters of your completed manuscript to ldpsubmissions@gmail.com. In the subject line add **Your Book's Title**. The manuscript must be in a Word Doc file and sent as an attachment. Document should be in Times New Roman, double spaced, and in size 12 font. Also, provide your synopsis and full contact information. If sending multiple submissions, they must each be in a separate email.

Have a story but no way to send it electronically? You can still submit to LDP/Ca$h Presents. Send in the first three chapters, written or typed, of your completed manuscript to:

LDP: Submissions Dept
P.O. Box 944
Stockbridge, GA 30281-9998

DO NOT send original manuscript. Must be a duplicate.
Provide your synopsis and a cover letter containing your full contact information.

Thanks for considering LDP and Ca$h Presents.

NEW RELEASES

BLOODLINE OF A SAVAGE 1&2
THESE VICIOUS STREETS 1&2
RELENTLESS GOON
RELENTLESS GOON 2
BY PRINCE A. TAUHID

THE BUTTERFLY MAFIA 1-3
BY FUMIYA PAYNE

A THUG'S STREET PRINCESS 1&2
BY MEESHA

CITY OF SMOKE 2
BY MOLOTTI

STEPPERS 1,2&3
THE REAL BADDIES OF CHI-RAQ
BY KING RIO

THE LANE 1&2
BY KEN-KEN SPENCE

THUG OF SPADES 1&2
LOVE IN THE TRENCHES 2
CORNER BOYS
BY COREY ROBINSON

TIL DEATH 3
BY ARYANNA

THE BIRTH OF A GANGSTER 4
BY DELMONT PLAYER

PRODUCT OF THE STREETS 1&2
BY DEMOND "MONEY" ANDERSON

NO TIME FOR ERROR
BY KEESE

MONEY HUNGRY DEMONS
BY TRANAY ADAMS

Coming Soon from Lock Down Publications/Ca$h Presents

IF YOU CROSS ME ONCE 6
ANGEL V
By Anthony Fields

IMMA DIE BOUT MINE 5
By Aryanna

A THUGS STREET PRINCESS 3
By Meesha

PRODUCT OF THE STREETS 3
By Demond Money Anderson

CORNER BOYS 2
By Corey Robinson

THE MURDER QUEENS 6&7
By Michael Gallon

CITY OF SMOKE 3
By Molotti

CONFESSIONS OF A DOPE BOY
By Nicholas Lock

THA TAKEOVER
By Keith Chandler

BETRAYAL OF A G 2
By Ray Vinci

CRIME BOSS
By Playa Ray

Available Now

RESTRAINING ORDER 1 & 2
By **CA$H & Coffee**

LOVE KNOWS NO BOUNDARIES 1-3
By **Coffee**

RAISED AS A GOON I, II, III & IV
BRED BY THE SLUMS I, II, III
BLAST FOR ME I & II
ROTTEN TO THE CORE I II III
A BRONX TALE I, II, III
DUFFLE BAG CARTEL I II III IV V VI
HEARTLESS GOON I II III IV V
A SAVAGE DOPEBOY I II
DRUG LORDS I II III
CUTTHROAT MAFIA I II
KING OF THE TRENCHES
By **Ghost**

LAY IT DOWN I & II
LAST OF A DYING BREED I II
BLOOD STAINS OF A SHOTTA I & II III
By **Jamaica**

LOYAL TO THE GAME I II III
LIFE OF SIN I, II III
By **TJ & Jelissa**

IF LOVING HIM IS WRONG…I & II
LOVE ME EVEN WHEN IT HURTS I II III
By **Jelissa**

PUSH IT TO THE LIMIT
By **Bre' Hayes**

BLOODY COMMAS I & II
SKI MASK CARTEL I, II & III
KING OF NEW YORK I II, III IV V
RISE TO POWER I II III
COKE KINGS I II III IV V
BORN HEARTLESS I II III IV
KING OF THE TRAP I II
By **T.J. Edwards**

WHEN THE STREETS CLAP BACK I & II III
THE HEART OF A SAVAGE I II III IV
MONEY MAFIA I II
LOYAL TO THE SOIL I II III
By **Jibril Williams**

A DISTINGUISHED THUG STOLE MY HEART I II & III
LOVE SHOULDN'T HURT I II III IV
RENEGADE BOYS 1-4
PAID IN KARMA 1-3
SAVAGE STORMS 1-3
AN UNFORESEEN LOVE 1-3
BABY, I'M WINTERTIME COLD 1-3
A THUG'S STREET PRINCESS 1&2
By **Meesha**

A GANGSTER'S CODE 1-3
A GANGSTER'S SYN 1-3
THE SAVAGE LIFE 1-3
CHAINED TO THE STREETS 1-3
BLOOD ON THE MONEY 1-3
A GANGSTA'S PAIN 1-3
BEAUTIFUL LIES AND UGLY TRUTHS
CHURCH IN THESE STREETS
By **J-Blunt**

CUM FOR ME 1-8
An LDP Erotica Collaboration

BLOOD OF A BOSS 1-5
SHADOWS OF THE GAME
TRAP BASTARD
By **Askari**

THE STREETS BLEED MURDER 1-3
THE HEART OF A GANGSTA 1-3
By **Jerry Jackson**

WHEN A GOOD GIRL GOES BAD
By **Adrienne**

THE COST OF LOYALTY 1-3
By **Kweli**

BRIDE OF A HUSTLA 1-3
THE FETTI GIRLS 1-3
CORRUPTED BY A GANGSTA 1-4
BLINDED BY HIS LOVE
THE PRICE YOU PAY FOR LOVE 1-3
DOPE GIRL MAGIC 1-3
By **Destiny Skai**

A KINGPIN'S AMBITION
A KINGPIN'S AMBITION II
I MURDER FOR THE DOUGH
By **Ambitious**

TRUE SAVAGE 1-7
DOPE BOY MAGIC 1-3
MIDNIGHT CARTEL 1-3
CITY OF KINGZ 1&2
NIGHTMARE ON SILENT AVE
THE PLUG OF LIL MEXICO 1&2
CLASSIC CITY
By **Chris Green**

A GANGSTER'S REVENGE 1-4
THE BOSS MAN'S DAUGHTERS 1-5
A SAVAGE LOVE 1&2
BAE BELONGS TO ME 1&2
A HUSTLER'S DECEIT 1-3
WHAT BAD BITCHES DO 1-3
SOUL OF A MONSTER 1-3
KILL ZONE
A DOPE BOY'S QUEEN 1-3
TIL DEATH 1-3
IMMA DIE BOUT MINE 1-4
By **Aryanna**

A DOPEBOY'S PRAYER
By **Eddie "Wolf" Lee**

THE KING CARTEL 1-3
By **Frank Gresham**

THESE NIGGAS AIN'T LOYAL 1-3
By **Nikki Tee**

GANGSTA SHYT 1-3
By **CATO**

THE ULTIMATE BETRAYAL
By **Phoenix**

BOSS'N UP 1-3
By **Royal Nicole**

I LOVE YOU TO DEATH
By **Destiny J**

I RIDE FOR MY HITTA
I STILL RIDE FOR MY HITTA
By **Misty Holt**

TENDER | KHUFU

LOVE & CHASIN' PAPER
By **Qay Crockett**

TO DIE IN VAIN
SINS OF A HUSTLA
By **ASAD**

BROOKLYN HUSTLAZ
By **Boogsy Morina**

BROOKLYN ON LOCK 1 & 2
By **Sonovia**

GANGSTA CITY
By **Teddy Duke**

A DRUG KING AND HIS DIAMOND 1-3
A DOPEMAN'S RICHES
HER MAN, MINE'S TOO 1&2
CASH MONEY HO'S
THE WIFEY I USED TO BE 1&2
PRETTY GIRLS DO NASTY THINGS
By **Nicole Goosby**

LIPSTICK KILLAH 1-3
CRIME OF PASSION 1-3
FRIEND OR FOE 1-3
By **Mimi**

TRAPHOUSE KING 1-3
KINGPIN KILLAZ 1-3
STREET KINGS 1&2
PAID IN BLOOD 1&2
CARTEL KILLAZ 1-3
DOPE GODS 1&2
By **Hood Rich**

THE STREETS ARE CALLING
By **Duquie Wilson**

STEADY MOBBN' 1-3
THE STREETS STAINED MY SOUL 1-3
By **Marcellus Allen**

WHO SHOT YA 1-3
SON OF A DOPE FIEND 1-4
HEAVEN GOT A GHETTO 1&2
SKI MASK MONEY 1&2
By **Renta**

GORILLAZ IN THE BAY 1-4
TEARS OF A GANGSTA 1/&2
3X KRAZY 1&2
STRAIGHT BEAST MODE 1&2
By **DE'KARI**

TRIGGADALE 1-3
MURDA WAS THE CASE 1-3
By **Elijah R. Freeman**

SLAUGHTER GANG 1-3
RUTHLESS HEART 1-3
By **Willie Slaughter**

GOD BLESS THE TRAPPERS 1-3
THESE SCANDALOUS STREETS 1-3
FEAR MY GANGSTA 1-5
THESE STREETS DON'T LOVE NOBODY 1-2
BURY ME A G 1-5
A GANGSTA'S EMPIRE 1-4
THE DOPEMAN'S BODYGAURD 1&2
THE REALEST KILLAZ 1-3
THE LAST OF THE OGS 1-3
By **Tranay Adams**

MARRIED TO A BOSS 1-3
By **Destiny Skai & Chris Green**

KINGZ OF THE GAME 1-7
CRIME BOSS 1-3
By **Playa Ray**

FUK SHYT
By **Blakk Diamond**

DON'T F#CK WITH MY HEART 1&2
By **Linnea**

ADDICTED TO THE DRAMA 1-3
IN THE ARM OF HIS BOSS
By **Jamila**

LOYALTY AIN'T PROMISED 1&2
By **Keith Williams**

YAYO 1-4
A SHOOTER'S AMBITION 1&2
BRED IN THE GAME
By **S. Allen**

TRAP GOD 1-3
RICH $AVAGE 1-3
MONEY IN THE GRAVE 1-3
CARTEL MONEY
By **Martell Troublesome Bolden**

FOREVER GANGSTA 1&2
GLOCKS ON SATIN SHEETS 1&2
By **Adrian Dulan**

TOE TAGZ 1-4
LEVELS TO THIS SHYT 1&2
IT'S JUST ME AND YOU
By **Ah'Million**

KINGPIN DREAMS 1-3
RAN OFF ON DA PLUG
By **Paper Boi Rari**

THE STREETS MADE ME 1-3
By **Larry D. Wright**

CONFESSIONS OF A GANGSTA 1-4
CONFESSIONS OF A JACKBOY 1-3
CONFESSIONS OF A HITMAN
By **Nicholas Lock**

I'M NOTHING WITHOUT HIS LOVE
SINS OF A THUG
TO THE THUG I LOVED BEFORE
A GANGSTA SAVED XMAS
IN A HUSTLER I TRUST
By **Monet Dragun**

QUIET MONEY 1-3
THUG LIFE 1-3
EXTENDED CLIP 1&2
A GANGSTA'S PARADISE
By **Trai'Quan**

CAUGHT UP IN THE LIFE 1-3
THE STREETS NEVER LET GO 1-3
By **Robert Baptiste**

NEW TO THE GAME 1-3
MONEY, MURDER & MEMORIES 1-3
By **Malik D. Rice**

CREAM 2-3
THE STREETS WILL TALK
By **Yolanda Moore**

THE STREETS WILL NEVER CLOSE 1-3
By **K'ajji**

LIFE OF A SAVAGE 1-4
A GANGSTA'S QUR'AN 1-4
MURDA SEASON 1-3
GANGLAND CARTEL 1-3
CHI'RAQ GANGSTAS 1-4
KILLERS ON ELM STREET 1-3
JACK BOYZ N DA BRONX 1-3
A DOPEBOY'S DREAM 1-3
JACK BOYS VS DOPE BOYS 1-3
COKE GIRLZ
COKE BOYS
SOSA GANG 1&2
BRONX SAVAGES
BODYMORE KINGPINS
BLOOD OF A GOON
By **Romell Tukes**

CONCRETE KILLA 1-3
VICIOUS LOYALTY 1-3
By **Kingpen**

THE ULTIMATE SACRIFICE 1-6
KHADIFI
IF YOU CROSS ME ONCE 1-3
ANGEL 1-4
IN THE BLINK OF AN EYE
By **Anthony Fields**

THE LIFE OF A HOOD STAR
By **Ca$h & Rashia Wilson**

NIGHTMARES OF A HUSTLA 1-3
BLOOD AND GAMES 1&2
By **King Dream**

GHOST MOB
By **Stilloan Robinson**

HARD AND RUTHLESS 1&2
MOB TOWN 251
THE BILLIONAIRE BENTLEYS 1-3
REAL G'S MOVE IN SILENCE
By **Von Diesel**

MOB TIES 1-7
SOUL OF A HUSTLER, HEART OF A KILLER 1-3
GORILLAZ IN THE TRENCHES
By **SayNoMore**

BODYMORE MURDERLAND 1-3
THE BIRTH OF A GANGSTER 1-4
By **Delmont Player**

FOR THE LOVE OF A BOSS 1&2
By **C. D. Blue**

KILLA KOUNTY 1-5
By **Khufu**

MOBBED UP 1-4
THE BRICK MAN 1-5
THE COCAINE PRINCESS 1-10
STEPPERS 1-3
SUPER GREMLIN 1-4
By **King Rio**

MONEY GAME 1&2
By **Smoove Dolla**

A GANGSTA'S KARMA 1-4
By **FLAME**

KING OF THE TRENCHES 1-3
By **GHOST & TRANAY ADAMS**

TENDER | KHUFU

QUEEN OF THE ZOO 1&2
By **Black Migo**

GRIMEY WAYS 1-3
BETRAYAL OF A G
By **Ray Vinci**

XMAS WITH AN ATL SHOOTER
By **Ca$h & Destiny Skai**

KING KILLA 1&2
By **Vincent "Vitto" Holloway**

BETRAYAL OF A THUG 1&2
By **Fre$h**

THE MURDER QUEENS 1-5
By **Michael Gallon**

FOR THE LOVE OF BLOOD 1-4
By **Jamel Mitchell**

HOOD CONSIGLIERE 1&2
NO TIME FOR ERROR
By **Keese**

PROTÉGÉ OF A LEGEND 1&2
LOVE IN THE TRENCHES 1&2
By **Corey Robinson**

THE PLUG'S RUTHLESS DAUGHTER
By **Tony Daniels**

BORN IN THE GRAVE 1-3
CRIME PAYS
By **Self Made Tay**

MOAN IN MY MOUTH
By **XTASY**

TORN BETWEEN A GANGSTER AND A GENTLEMAN
By **J-BLUNT & Miss Kim**

LOYALTY IS EVERYTHING 1-3
CITY OF SMOKE 1&2
By **Molotti**

HERE TODAY GONE TOMORROW 1&2
By **Fly Rock**

WOMEN LIE MEN LIE 1-4
FIFTY SHADES OF SNOW 1-3
STACK BEFORE YOU SPLURGE
GIRLS FALL LIKE DOMINOES
NAÏVE TO THE STREETS
By **ROY MILLIGAN**

PILLOW PRINCESS
By **S. Hawkins**

THE BUTTERFLY MAFIA 1-3
SALUTE MY SAVAGERY 1&2
By **Fumiya Payne**

THE LANE 1&2
By Ken-Ken Spence

THE PUSSY TRAP 1-5
By **Nene Capri**

DIRTY DNA
By **Blaque**

SANCTIFIED AND HORNY
by **XTASY**

BOOKS BY LDP'S CEO, CA$H

TRUST IN NO MAN
TRUST IN NO MAN 2
TRUST IN NO MAN 3
BONDED BY BLOOD
SHORTY GOT A THUG
THUGS CRY
THUGS CRY 2
THUGS CRY 3
TRUST NO BITCH
TRUST NO BITCH 2
TRUST NO BITCH 3
TIL MY CASKET DROPS
RESTRAINING ORDER
RESTRAINING ORDER 2
IN LOVE WITH A CONVICT
LIFE OF A HOOD STAR
XMAS WITH AN ATL SHOOTER